CW00471736

"Powerfully voices the conc
tenderness and sensitivity. M(
perspective in a way that is t(
He is a consistently thoughtfu.
His prose moves seamlessly between pensive introspection and
meticulous observation, lyricism and drama."
Andrew Crumey, Man Booker Longlisted author of Mr Mee.

"A great read. Set against the vibrant backdrop of the 1990s
London music scene, "Dead Rock Stars" is a mesmerising
study of grief as well as a coming of age novel. I found myself
immersed in the narratives of Jeff and Emma and marvelled at
how the author captured both voices with such authenticity,
particularly that of the self-destructive young woman."
Ruth Dugdall, bestselling author.

"Exciting, evocative and one of the most emotive pieces
I've read. Very powerful. Packs a punch."
Sara Hawys Roberts, author of Withdrawn Traces:
Searching For The Truth About Richey Manic.

"A deft exploration of that all-defining bond between siblings.
This book will break your heart. And then rebuild it."
Sarah Dobbs, author of The Sea Inside Me.

"Mankowski builds a compelling story from the inside out, by
holding subtle facets of relationships up to the light and
exploring them with lapidarian precision. Even in the midst of
its clubs and rock bands, the novel maintains a thoughtful
serenity throughout, albeit one with sparkling touches of wit.
A cracking read."
John Schoneboom, award winning author of Fontoon.

"This is incredible – I love Emma's voice and think she is
brilliant. I could not empathise more with her, and I think a lot
of girls will identify with and understand her. Manages to
capture a really authentic young female voice, which for
a male writer is no mean feat."
Rachael Charlotte, poet.

"Dead Rock Stars"

Guy Mankowski

www.darkstroke.com

Discover us online:
www.darkstroke.com

Join us on instagram:
www.instagram.com/darkstrokebooks/

Include **#darkstroke** in a photo of yourself
holding this book on Instagram and
something nice will happen.

This book is dedicated to my parents

About the Author

Guy Mankowski was singer in the signed band Alba Nova, and went on to play guitar in bands like The Beautiful Machine. His novels include 'The Intimates' (a 2011 Read Regional Title), 'Letters from Yelena' (winner of an Arts Council Literature award & featured in GCSE training by Osiris Educational), 'How I Left The National Grid' (written as part of a PhD in Creative Writing) and 'An Honest Deceit' (winner of an Arts Council Literature Award and a New Writing North Read Regional Award).

He is a full-time lecturer at The University of Lincoln.

Acknowledgements

More than any other book I've written, this is the one that has meant the most to me. Throughout the years that I worked on this book it went through many changes. It would not have been completed without lots of feedback from various talented writers. I'd like to thank Sara Hawys Roberts, Rachael Charlotte and Hollie Martorella, who offered great feedback on early drafts, as well as Cassandre Balasso-Bardin. I'd like to thank Dona Bell. I'd like to thank Roberta Louise Green and Lou Woodcont for being there in the way they have been, in good times and bad- and not only when it suited them. The support of my family was most important and so I offer my thanks for Vivienne and Andrew Mankowski. I'd also like to thank Laurence for his editing and all the team at darkstroke for their input.

"Dead
Rock Stars"

Chapter One

The only time I saw Emma play a proper gig was in August 1999. I would replay it in my mind so many times.

It's a hot night, and the summer holidays have peaked. They're coming to an end, and the retreating crowds in Camden prove that. There are few bodies around the Tube when Mum and I get off and walk down the high street. Hippies in plaid trousers. Stalls selling sunglasses, bad replica t-shirts of bands I've not heard of. Truth be told, I'm scared, and as I pass my reflection in a shop window, I see a boy with terrified eyes, a single multi-coloured braid in his long, dirty, blonde hair. Mum is fighting a clear sense of disdain. She removes her Gucci sunglasses with perfectly polished nails. Her Dior perfume is like industrial strength air freshener in this backdrop of hemp and skunkweed. I know these smells because of Emma. The idea was always that I wouldn't become too familiar. Mum is scared that going to this gig will make me all the more enthralled by my sister's lifestyle when she is here to attempt to cleave her from it. But Emma has won the battle for my innocence that she waged with our parents, as we're on her turf tonight.

Near the lock, the fresh orange juice stall churns bright globes into pulp. The vinyls on the stalls we pass are trapped worlds of possibility. Around the lock, punks sit at sticky benches, legs lolled over the wall. I wonder if there'll be many girls at the gig. "We can't be far off it now," Mum says, and I notice stress lines at the corners of her mouth.

"The venue is called The Purple Turtle," I answer.

Mum winces at a man playing a djembe on the pavement. "Venue, please," she says. "More like den of iniquity."

We realise we should've got off at Camden Town. Mum has

never walked this far, at least for as long as I can remember. The venue is on a busy corner, and outside the queue is a straggle of threadbare boa and dulled leather. Plastic jewels sparkle on wrists, and makeup is yet to crinkle.

"I'm going to attempt to find myself a passable glass of wine," Mum says, as we move inside. Her handbag is at the crook of her elbow. "I stress the word *attempt*."

"Can I have a beer? This is a gig. And my mother is with me."

"No. You'll have a coke and you'll enjoy it."

She heads for the bar, reeking of self-regarding afternoons in John Lewis. She smells like parental rallying at sports day, and post-argument sulks with Dad. At the bar I overhear her ask the barman for a "white zinfandel". The barman says, "I'm sorry, but we don't have any pale ales." My mother looks at him as if he is a cat who has just cocked its leg and peed directly on her foot. As the barman turns away from her, she hisses the word 'shithole' with a passion that sounds like it's come from the bottom of her soul.

I see a raised stage and on it a lithe, ratty man wears an open waistcoat to show off his six-pack. He reminds me of a lizard. Behind him the keyboard honks and the guitarist makes his instrument sound like a buzz saw. "We're Portal and this is our next single," he says over the noise. I realise that they're not sound checking. This is it. The night has already started.

A hollow-eyed girl in a leopard print coat is sat in front of a desk on which I can see various Cherub-related items. There are pink powder compacts with their heart-shaped logo on front, a white ballerina music box with their name emblazoned on it in red, a set of posters, tied with pink ribbons, and marbled vinyls fanned out on top of postcards of the band. I begin to appreciate how hard Emma has worked, crafting the world of her music.

There's a knot of people at the front, a few feet back from the stage, and Cherub come on. My first sight of Emma is announced by Mum who says, in a low panic, "there she is."

I look up to see Emma on the steps by the stage, bending over to check her black Telecaster, before darting out of a fire exit. She is wearing a black baby doll dress with a white Peter Pan collar and black Mary Janes with frilly white socks. In her bleach blonde hair, a silver tiara is nestling.

Her guitarist, Melissa, and her drummer, Donna, stay on stage and seem to debate something for ages while Melissa fiddles with an amp. Their hunched body language is unnervingly fixed. I decide there is a technical problem that, by the looks of it, is insurmountable. I sense Mum's impending triumph and the way she'll revel in it. All middle-class elbows and triumphant phone calls while Emma stays in the background looking irreversibly bruised.

"You alright?" I ask Mum as she sips her wine. She blanches.

"The band would look a bit more professional if they stayed offstage until the set started," she says.

"Emma's not on stage," I say, sipping my coke.

"I hope she puts loo paper on the seat before she sits down in places like this. Don't tell anyone you're her brother if you're asked. You're too young to be in here, and I don't need the new school finding out."

This remark annoys me on so many levels. Some pretty girls in vintage fur are standing near the stage. I'd have loved the chance to play the role of the innocent younger brother. Mum's expression suggests she *sees* this thought in my mind. "Not a word, Jeff," she says. "You'll have plenty of time to hang out in places like this when you're older, if you decide this is how you want to live."

I have already decided this is how I want to live but am sharp enough not to admit that. When Cherub do come on stage, it's gradual enough to betray their amateurism. My heart beats, hard. Emma's eyes are lined with thick dark kohl, and it gives them a shine and lustre, an eminence I've not seen before. Certainly not during the mornings she sat in her bay window, all bruised legs and missing strings, chopping at her acoustic guitar. But tonight, she's transformed.

A loud buzz emanates from Emma's guitar as she puts the lead in, to a light smatter of applause. She checks the input and laughs at something Donna says as she twirls drumsticks. I realise her band are wearing identical white mink dresses, but the bassist is wearing a fake fur leopard print stole over her shoulder. It's like all the best items in a vintage store have been selectively thieved by them. For a moment I question if that might've been exactly what Emma has done. She's always been the sort of person that could put on anything strange you find in those shops and make them look sensational.

"We're Cherub," Emma says.

Mum clears her throat. A few people look at her, but Mum looks ahead, determined not to acknowledge that she cleared her throat a little too loud.

The drums start. The fuzzy bass that joins it is so loud. Emma saws her guitar, and distorted chords make the sound like thick, treacly sludge. When Emma sings, the first few words are lost, then when her voice is caught by the mike, Mum jumps theatrically. A voice that sounds a little bit too much like her when she's arguing soon becomes a grizzled, Courtney Love style lament. But in soft bits there's a curl to her words that is unique.

They churn through a twenty-minute set. I can't hear a word of it. It's all vowels-'ow,' 'yargh' and 'ee'. I wonder what the point of all that lyric writing was. At one point a couple of the girls pogo, until one of them dramatically forces another to stop using the single word, "*Embarrassing*".

Emma winces, snarls. She pouts, leaning over her guitar when she's not singing, and tries to hide that she can't quite make some of the chords. I think of her rehearsing in the boathouse and suspect that, in her nervousness, she has just forgotten how to play a whole verse.

During the smattering of applause, she glances over at us for one intense second. Mum blushes and looks ashamed. Once or twice the music takes flight and Emma and Melissa face each other, chopping at their guitars in time. Their red nails flash as they slice at the strings. In one song, Emma attempts a star-jump. The bassist pulls the tiara from Emma's head during a solo and places it on her own. It lodges at the back of her hair during the final number, which some of the audience sing along to. For almost all of the last song the

6

words are nearly audible. I keep thinking of the way that, a few nights before, Emma had rifled through my notebook for lines, and had scribbled a few in her own journal. Has she already sung them without me realising? Or did she decide they were puerile, and forget them out a few hours later?

But something clicks into place, and her words finally cut straight through to us. She sings, "Courtney's new single / Is titled Bulimia / I sing along / Whilst I cut my arms."

I look over at Mum, who tries to hide a gulp. With a slight smile on her lips, as if she knows we can hear her, Emma sings, "Princess Diana / Tarred and feathered / Dragged right down / Kensington High Street / Such an apt / Climax to her funeral / I'm The Sculptress."

Mum has gone pale. The song clatters to an end, a cacophony of missed notes and late drum hits. "That was our new single, The Sculptress. We've been Cherub. Good night, Camden," she says.

They leave the stage. Mum finishes her wine. "So that's that then," she says.

"I thought they were good," I answer, anticipating Mum's itinerary of complaints. But she just winces, and I see that her lipstick has touched her teeth. "Maybe we should have forked out for singing lessons after all," she says, looking past me.

One of the girls in the knot at the front leans over the cage and stretches her fingers, reaching for their set list. A tech comes over, prises it off, and hands it to her. As mum clatters to her feet, the girl clutches the set list to her heart. She's wearing the exact same tiara that Emma had worn onstage.

"Right. Let's go. Before Emma catches something," Mum snaps.

Chapter Two

I didn't think of myself as a damaged person that summer, but my parents clearly did. Even for a couple of people that saw the world as their own massive playground, they managed to pick up on that. Sending me to the Isle of Wight for that summer was all to do with my sister dying nine months before. I thought about it a lot on the train down. As England, wet, green and clenched into its suburbs, flashed by in the windows. I was wearing a blue silk shirt that Emma had once owned, and the fact that I wore little else that summer spoke volumes.

Once the decision had been made for me to spend the summer with friends, Mum started flipping through her mental Rolodex of all the families that might take me on for the summer. During the probable ten seconds Mum thought about it, she decided that even though the best friend I'd had in my home village was, in her words, 'a total liability', his parents were the only ones bohemian enough to agree to take me on. Her opinion of River was cemented the second time he was suspended from school for inexplicably setting fire to a bush. It was an incident he tended to refer to affectionately as his 'arson charge'. Then there was my dad's view of him, neatly summarised by the time he pulled me to one side and said, "Why do you and this boy need to spend so much time together, precisely?" But for all her disdain, my mother's need to get rid of me trumped any concern she might have had.

After deciding Emma and I had completed our childhoods, the island was abandoned by both of them. To them it was a toxic waste ground, the place where words like 'nervous breakdown' and 'heroin' had first entered our families vocabulary. It didn't occur to them that having a Dad that was only interested in his yacht and his mistress, and a Mum that couldn't stop competing with her daughter might've had anything to with what happened to Emma. To them it was all about *England,* and the only thing left to salvage was what was left of their marriage. Presumably I was just a fragment of the aftermath, and beyond saving. Even then I suspected Emma would do more to save me than they would.

From what I had gathered at boarding school, their new life comprised choosing Koi ponds and getting into Feng Shui, and whatever else they thought would fill the void. But even they saw that they couldn't take me out of a boarding school and onto a summer in the Far East. They knew that at least on the Isle of Wight I was kind of a *somebody*, even if it was only because I was *somebody's brother*.

Emma had been on the verge of something great though. I had known it, and it had made me scared of her. When I passed her bedroom on her way to mine I would see her naked, bruised legs pulled up against her in the window, and I would catch the faint smell of menthol cigarettes, and know that if I caught a glimpse of her I would see a woman in pain. As she played her guitar, dirty ringlets framed her face, her summer dress falling off her shoulders. What Emma really found easy was looking cool. If you went to a vintage shop with her and there was a dress on the mannequin that most people would feel stupid in, she'd put it on and bring it to life in a way you couldn't imagine. You kind of wanted to get your picture taken with her because she looked that good.

I closed my eyes and tried to shut out the train guards announcement so I could picture Emma's face. But, for some reason, it wasn't coming to me, and I was livid with myself for that and for not doing more about her unhappiness. Perhaps reading her diary was only going to make me feel worse, I thought.

When she'd died that November the loneliness of her death had felt strangely at odds with how much attention she'd been getting. It seemed strange that no one knew exactly what had happened to her, given that they had spent so much time talking about Emma. She had a record deal, and there'd just been this mysterious six months where she went from a nobody to being regularly in the music weeklies. It had all started with her moving to Camden. She began wearing baby doll dresses and silver tiaras and she wrote angry messages on her body with eyeliner. The messages got angrier as the drugs got harder. I would get my news about her from copies of NME in the village corner shop on the weekends they let us out of school and into the local village. I just couldn't believe the music weeklies were interviewing my sister. And she would say things in those features that I didn't understand-all those references to 'chasing the dragon'. One minute it was all a big joke and the next Mum was slumped in the armchair in the hallway, holding the receiver a few inches from her ear as if unable to believe what she had just been told. She was unable to speak, and I knew, at that moment, that I'd lost my sister.

I was conscious that, buried at the bottom of my rucksack was the one object that might answer the big question on my mind. How had Emma ended up dying? The diary I had found in her bag a few weeks after her death was bound to reveal what had really been going on from her perspective. I knew the legal verdict, and all the stupid conclusions that the court came to, but not what had been really going on in her life during those final months to take her to that point. My mother had carefully screened me from the truth-there had been no newspapers in the house during the aftermath. I wondered if she had been trying to even conceal the truth from herself, and that was why she hadn't tried to crack the lock on the diary. Was she worried about what Emma would reveal? Perhaps that's why I didn't tell her when I found the key to it, in the lining of her bag. And despite dying to know, I had so far been unable to bring myself to read those diary pages. I just knew they would answer all my questions and, in some way, perhaps I didn't want that. Not yet.

I had only ever flicked through that book, glanced at those dense lines, at the way she had filled every inch of the pages with the contents of her mind. But something had stopped me delving into it. Was I scared it would admit something I couldn't deal with? Was I scared it would reveal that she hadn't really cared about me? I knew one day I would have to read it. But something told me that I would need to go back to my old home in order to do so. Every night, when I closed my eyes, I saw the same thing; that wooden coffin, polished and far too slender, at the altar of the church. They all seemed so sure my sister was in it, even if I just couldn't believe that.

I was still thinking about these things when I got off the hovercraft on the island, walked along the beach under the shimmering sun, and stood on the road by the sea wall. It loomed over the pontoon where River said he'd meet me.

It was a small village built around the sailing club, which was embedded on a circular sea wall high above the ocean. Deep tanned men, wearing life jackets and expensive deck shoes, were spilling out from it. The sailors congratulated each other as they came out of the club and into the pub behind me. They all had sunglasses with red cords around the backs of their necks, and I kept hearing the word 'yah'.

Some Sloane Square mother in Gucci sunglasses threw me onto the pavement as she roared past in a Chelsea Tractor, her fixed smile refusing to acknowledge my existence. I tried to shut out the sailing club crowd, and not be distracted by the rows of young girls sipping soft drinks and swinging their legs further down the sea wall. Unfortunately I knew my old friend too well, and wondered if, despite his parents' giving permission for me to stay, he would really bother to come and meet me. If not, I decided I would have to sleep on the beach for the summer. River was someone for whom the necessity of one day became a distant memory the next.

I heard the sound of wood splintering.

A beaten-up wooden dinghy had smashed its nose into the bottom of the pontoon. I recognised the shock of sandy blonde hair, shot through with multi-coloured braids. A skinny boy was surveying the damage he'd just caused to his own boat. "River!" I shouted.

The commotion caused everyone on the pavement nearby to rush and look at what the noise was all about.

"What *are* you doing?" I shouted.

River squinted up at the line of spectators and gave a sharp naval salute. "I was doing a Baywatch landing. Permission to come aboard?"

Some of the young girls sat on the sea wall tittered at this. There was the kind of confused admiration River tended to provoke. "You need a permit to land here, sport," said a passing sailing instructor.

"My dad's the Commodore of the club," River said, bounding up the jetty.

A complete lie.

I looked down at his boat, now lassoed with an old piece of rope to the pontoon.

"And that's my rescue vehicle?" I said.

"Don't knock the Brown Owl," he answered. "She can move when she has to."

"When's that? I thought these dinghies were supposed to be made of Formica, not wood."

"It's old school. It's never let me down. It's my Old Maud. Now grab something from the sailing club buffet and let's get out of this place before someone sees me."

"We're going back to yours in that thing?"

"Try and get some of their frittata. The salmon. The *hors d'oeuvres*," he said, fishing out his penknife.

"We're really sailing all the way round to Bembridge in that?"

"Yes. But we've got to catch the tide. Shift yourself!"

Chapter Three

The Brown Owl sloshed through the morning sunshine and I wondered how this heap of shining oil, splintered wood and fading rope had ever proved seaworthy, let alone capable of taking us a quarter of the way round the island.

I tried to remember what I could about sailing. River got me to transfer the small red sail at the front to the other side whenever he tacked to go in a new direction. After, he'd tie each rope off and put his bony feet up, before pulling out a Marlboro Light. He reminded me of those bits in the Beano where Dennis The Menace would come home from school and put his feet in a bowl of hot water as he tucked into a dish of bangers and mash.

"You really think we're on course?"

He winced at me. "If your fannying about with the bread rolls hasn't cost us, we'll have beaten the tide."

"That woman in the café said it wasn't open even though she was serving the older men as she said it."

"They see you as an oik," River said. "Boys like us, we are shit on their shoe until we get old enough to marry their daughters. They're only interested in our *sperm*."

"And what if we don't make it round in time?"

"We'll be marooned off Priory Beach and won't get round the rocks 'til night-time."

"In which case we really are in trouble. You could have told me you were coming by boat."

"How? By sending a carrier pigeon?"

It was a good point.

He jumped up and ran to the front of the boat. "I just saw a thresher shark."

"Unlikely," I said.

He turned, squinting as he puffed at the cigarette. His fringe was in his eyes, dirty and blonde. I'd always envied the fact that his parents let him grow his hair long. It made him look feral.

"Do your parents not give you grief about your hair?" I said, thinking of boarding school.

He threw himself to his feet before leaning against the mast. He went on to one foot. The boat was bobbing hard on the waves, and I secretly marvelled at his balance.

"They haven't seen me in weeks. They are away for most of the summer. Botswana. That's why they're okay with you staying in the annexe. They've left *Ruth* in charge."

I thought of River's bookish older sister and wondered what power struggles there'd been between the two of them. "Annexe?" I asked. "You mean I've got my own room?"

"No. You've got your own wing of the house."

Once we'd tacked inland, the water off the coast of Bembridge was smooth and clear. I looked down at shallow waters, at barely submerged rocks covered in barnacles. I thought about the long stretch of smooth beach where my mind had gambolled during our last months on the island. I looked out at the thin rows of hard, smooth pebbles, the little patches of clay, and above the beach the rich green vegetation. I decided that if River got too much for me I could still camp in those woods, or in the quiet inlet between the Baywatch Café and Priory beach. I'd need a tent, though.

River walked up the middle of the road, barefoot. He had the walk of a person who looked as if they might go into any doorway. I remembered that even though walking barefoot was the done thing on this part of the island, he was always a touch too reckless. He'd walk up the middle of the road even when a car was coming at him, and refuse to get out the way for anyone. It was as if he was playing chicken with the whole world.

He threw a stick into an overhead apple tree and chased the fruit as it rolled down the road. I watched as he ran ahead of me. He jumped onto walls and darted along them. When a bus passed at the end of the road, he launched the apple at it, and it glanced over the top deck as it flashed by. When we passed a letterbox, he jumped up and gobbed into it. When we passed a phone box he ran in, threw himself against the interior, then picked up the receiver and spat on it. There was no outlet for his energies. When there was nothing else for him to jump on, he told me about a bomb he'd made from old batteries that could "blow someone's arm off". When I asked how he got hold of that many batteries he said, "My girlfriend's dad owns a factory that makes them."

At the time, none of it felt like lies. I felt such a rush of relief to have my friend back, and to be here, to be walking up the street where I had lived as a child. I thought of the mornings I had laid in my bed there, Emma asleep in the next room, when I had felt so safe, with the sound of the owls in the leaves, and the ocean at the end of the street.

Sunlight poured through the trees that bordered the road. It felt as if it was so long since I'd been here. Ahead of me, bathed in the falling white, was a young woman in red shorts, trailing a handbag. With her sultry walk and her poise, she transfixed me, before disappearing into one of the driveways. One moment she was here, the next she was gone. It reminded me of the sight of Emma, guitar on her back, walking to River's house for band practice in their boathouse. The sense of magic I had felt during my childhood, when I lived on this street, came swimming back. It was like the sensation you get from a gulp of red wine on a late summer afternoon, one that dissolves your whole sense of time.

I caught River by the arm. "It's really good to hang out and to get to go for a walk together," I said in a moment of bliss.

He pulled a face. "Men don't go for walks together, Jeff," he said. "That's what you do with your girlfriend."

He ran ahead of me, and I smiled.

Chapter Four

I remember the moment I walked down the driveway, right towards the lawn of River's house. It felt like the promised land, this little haven bordered by trees. Sunlight came over the house and blasted the garden with a white light at the moment I saw Ruth.

She was lying on the grass in a pinstriped summer dress, one bare foot kicking upwards. Her head was in a book. As we walked closer, the dark bob of hair turned to look at me. Ruth's face had changed so much since I'd last seen her that I barely recognised it. I hadn't realised her eyes were so dark, or that she had a Cindy Crawford mole. Ruth's eyes widened when she saw me. "Hello, Jeff," she said in a voice that sounded measured.

I remembered the last time we'd spoken. It was after school, when I'd gone down to the sea to swim, leaving my school clothes on a rock. I had been drying my hair on my shirt sleeve as I'd walked to the top of the stone steps. She was sat on a bench overlooking the beach. We'd smiled at each other, but I hadn't felt able to ask how long she'd been there for. We had been two people, pressed too deep in our angst-ridden worlds to communicate.

If the Collins' house was a person, it would be a woman in her forties who runs yoga classes in a kaftan. River had a large room overlooking the back lawn. He'd filled it with graphic novels, soft pornography and various musical instruments. A large drum kit in the corner had a guitar resting against it. I started trying to tune his Telecaster. I knew that his sister was listening through the open window below us as we jammed around a groove. It felt summery and dusty and I wanted to live inside it. I don't know if you can live inside a rattling song, but on days like that I tried to. When we stopped singing, I heard Ruth humming from outside and tried to figure out what she was thinking. She always seemed to keep her distance. I wondered if it was because of the afternoon River and I had thrown water bombs at the top decks of passing buses from the attic room. I tried to work out why I thought of her as being made from the same stuff as me.

That evening, in a small living room by the garden porch, River and I sat down to watch Friends. As I watched the screen, I thought about how those characters in New York came from a totally different world. Their camaraderie, their bohemian vibe, the fact that they got each other's jokes, and all lived in the same bubble. I was used to conversations being brittle and brief. I was used to people never really getting each other or doing so for a bit and then disappearing. A blue kind of darkness was descending outside when Ruth threw herself on the armchair next to me. She had a small pot of chocolate ice cream in her hand.

"Don't you dare change the channel," she said. "I've been waiting for Friends all week."

"If you were that bothered, you wouldn't have missed the start," River said.

"Oh, shut up, River," she said, her voice sounding posh.

In a tense kind of arrangement, the three of us chortled at the same points, as if we wouldn't dare not acknowledge the witticisms.

"I think Jeff fancies Monica," River said during an advert.

I could feel Ruth's eyes on the side of my face. I could tell I was going red.

"No, I don't," I said, even though I kind of did.

Ruth smiled, and dug her fork into her ice cream. I didn't understand her expression. It was as if someone had tried to make fun of her. She scoffed. "So Jeff likes them skinny then," she said.

"You have the same hairstyle as her," I said.

I don't know where the remark came from, but was pleased with her reaction. Ruth offered a strange smile, as if she had decided not to fall for a certain trick. She curled her legs up against her chest. I tried to decide if that mole was pretty or not.

"But I don't have the same life," she said, without taking her eyes off the screen. "I live in a huge house with an unhinged younger brother, with nothing to do all summer except study and try to control *him*."

"Dramatic," River said.

She looked at me with her brown eyes, and their intensity was startling. "But you won't give me any trouble, will you, Jeff?" she asked.

Chapter Five

I had only ever flitted past this part of the house, but once I'd inserted the key and opened the door it seemed to exhale in welcome for me. It sounded so, so empty. A hallway of whitewashed, wooden floors, bedrooms on either side of it. I went into one on the left, which looked out onto the gravel driveway, bordered with trees. The cupboards and wardrobes all had opened doors, revealing their bare interiors.

There was a strange feel to the annexe, as if you could sense the ghosts of previous tenants. You could almost hear them.

Annexe, I thought. On the side. Like I am.

Having a totally clear space for myself was something I'd never had. I found myself, as if enacting a ritual, unpacking the meagre contents of my rucksack. But it was taking out Emma's diary, and placing it under the window, that told me something. It said that *now* was the time to open it. I had been given time, space, silence.

I had no more excuses.

Something really weird happened the moment I had that realisation. I still can't explain it. I sat down on the floor and just started crying like a baby. A torrent came out of me. At school I'd never had a moment when someone wouldn't have heard me if I'd cried. And I must have really backed all this stuff up. It was just pouring out of me in this very still and quiet setting-a place that made my crying seem even louder. All this huge emotion, and the only thing observing me was this empty driveway. For a moment I questioned if the stones in the gravel were like a kind of audience, and if they were as dumbfounded by what was coming out of me.

I could actually see the water from the tears making puddles on the dusty wood floor. I kept wiping it away before another huge splosh followed. My hands were wet, my arms were wet, and my face was wet. And all the time I was looking at Emma's diary and thinking how if I opened it, this would just be the start. And then I had this other thought, which became kind of like a mantra. I somehow felt like it was already too late, and that it was going to go on to be even later. I even said it out loud, like the windowpane and the gravel would care what I had to say. I was thinking that they were watching me, but Emma was not. Something told me she could *hear* me. But I had no idea what I wanted to say to her.

Realising there was nothing left to lose made me stop thinking about it and just open the damn thing.

It struck me what a piece of art her diary was. The intricate pattern on the white faux marble exterior hinted at the lavish ivory sheets inside, but the thick volume was full of surprises. The italicised handwriting, filling every corner of the page, was titled only by written digits. Between these fine-written entries were images she'd stuck in: Oscar Wilde, with his eyes gouged out by biro marks, Sylvia Plath sunbathing, happy, with lyrics written around her, including the words, "DON'T BELIEVE HIM, SYLVIA". There were cuttings of Emma's reviews, pictures of Emma onstage, surrounded in swirls of red paint. The undercurrents within these people's personas, with all their secret tragedy and betrayal, brought to the surface by swathes of red and blue paint, dried, thick enough to pick at, visceral. The paint expanded certain pages, and shrivelled others.

Were these dreams, visions, or just an expression of something that Emma had felt she had to get down? The back pages of the diary were full of lists of things Emma had had to buy for the band: cables, batteries for her effects pedals, plectrums. I realised this was not just her Final Will and Testament. It was an itinerary of her life as an artist. She had hand-drawn fliers. The pasted backstage passes and articles, of her band as well as Adam's, showed someone trying to move into the world of their imagination.

As I flicked through it, I realised that she had really started this diary in the months leading up to her death. I was not surprised that the entries had become longer and longer. Had she intuited, on some level, that an ending was coming? Had this made her want to set down her thoughts before she left? Either way, I was so glad I had taken the chance to go into her room and seek this thing out during the aftermath.

I sat down, cross-legged, feeling all the tears dry on my body. I decided that over the summer I would work through these pages, absorbing all they had to tell me. I knew there would be shocks, revelations, maybe even an explanation of her death.

Why would a diary be private unless it had power?

I knew it also had the power in *some* way to revive her. People whose dear ones have departed carry locks of hair or photos of them in a favourite moment. I think we want to carry keys that can unlock our version of these people again.

The first page was a picture of Frances Farmer facing a drawing of Ophelia, beautiful and dying amongst the weeds. My sister's psychic accomplices were all tragic figures.

The diary started with some pages she'd stuck in from another journal. The date told me she'd written it when she was fourteen. Younger than me.

The sun woke me up at five am. As I couldn't sleep I decided to creep out and go down to the sea.

I just stood there watching it, but something told me I had to go into the water. Even though the sun was bright, the water was cold, and I waded in until it reached my waist.

To my surprise, the ocean spoke to me. The waves said, "Hello, Emma. I was expecting you."

In shock, I whispered, "I didn't know you could speak, much less expect anyone!"

She smiled. "You know a lot more than you like to admit to people. I see a lot of people come to visit the sea, but I have noticed you, Emma."

"What's so special about me?" I said, rubbing my eyes.

"You see things other people don't," she said. "You see through people and situations and you feel things in people that others don't. You know what I am talking about?"

"When I'm playing music, do you mean?"

The voice grew stronger. "When you are doing anything."

I didn't understand what was happening. I felt so frustrated that I wanted to cry. "I don't feel like I'm doing anything," I said. "I don't even know why I am on this planet."

"The point of you being here is to simply be here. Every stone that ends up on the beach I have placed there for a reason. And you are no different, Emma. You are young and headstrong, and you sometimes allow yourself to believe that you have nothing to offer. But I would not have invited you here to speak with me if that was true."

I couldn't believe it. Why would the sea pick me of all people, the girl who is too scared to put her hand up and even speak out in class, in case people realise how stupid she is?

"You have a spirit that is very special, Emma," she said. "An ability to get others to open up. You will inspire people."

"How?" I asked, looking into the waves.

"It won't be at all easy, but you are on the right path. You need to look to the love you feel for people. You need to see what goes on around you and turn it into art, even if you think it won't ever reach people. And if you do, Emma, I promise, you will make more of an impact on the world than you even thought possible."

I had so many questions. Had this wonderful being really found the right person?

Somehow in my bones I knew it had. But before I had the chance to thank the sea, she said, "I am always here if you need me. I am just a few steps away."

And then she was gone!

I walked home in a daze.

Chapter Six

When I finished reading it, I realised I was finding it hard to breathe. I could see why she had kept this entry and put it in the front of her diary. I had never been able to put into words what was so special about her and there, in some strange way, it was, written down. I had always been looking in the wrong places.

It reassured me. I wasn't wrong to think she was so unique just because she had been my sister. I knew there was so much more to it than that.

This is the sister I knew, I thought, the one I first knew as a little boy, who pushed me on the swings, who made up games with me in the garden where she insisted we pretend to be fairies and gnomes. She drew pictures with me using brightly coloured crayons in the drawing room during endless, sun-drenched afternoons. Before boys. Before *drugs*. I felt so grateful that something existed which reminded me of the real Emma.

And that set me off again.

I wasn't even worried about River hearing me, although I knew that if he did, he'd either ignore it or bring it up in some devastating moment in the future. But I think part of me *wanted* someone to hear the crying. I remember thinking if Ruth came through the door at that moment it might be the only thing that could make me feel a bit better. And you know the weird thing? As soon as I started crying again, all this other stuff came out. Through the childish sobbing I started saying things like, "Dad doesn't care, and Mum just wants to control what everyone thinks." And stuff like, "And that's what started the whole thing."

I was actually looking at my reflection in the windowpane

and saying things to my strange, clown-like face. "My parents don't want me, and River only wants me around until he realises I'm not cool. And I'm all on my own and Emma's in the ground all because of some prick. And I just want to die." And when I said 'die', it made me feel even worse. I heard this weird stirring somewhere else in the house and then I *really* wanted Ruth to come through the door if only to say, "What are you, the picture of Dorian Gray?" or some other clever literary reference I wasn't smart enough to get.

All the pain of the past joined together like a horrible story, growing louder and louder in those empty rooms. It was like I was being forced to say the story out loud just to get it out of me. And even then, I knew that wouldn't change anything. I found myself saying, over and over, "You are so screwed." In that state I couldn't even imagine anything good ever happening. Like anyone ever fancying me or loving me. Why would a skinny boy with a stupid braid in his hair be of interest to anyone? I felt sure that everyone would just fall at the first hurdle when they got to know me, before giving up.

At that point, I was breathing all heavy and watching my face with the shoulders going up and down. I wasn't even able to control that anymore. But I wiped my eyes and stood up. And I said, "Well, it's already too late. You might as well read on."

It was good to hear her voice in my head as I began the first proper entry. It was kind of like having her with me. I wasn't alone, even in the annexe. I was back with the Emma I had known.

The entry was titled, '08'.

Everything is coming to a head. So, in an attempt to prove his devotion to me, Jay bought a ticket to a PJ Harvey gig in London a few weeks ago. It set me on a collision course with Mum. The gig was on a school night but, of course, despite all the repercussions I still went. Even now, two weeks later, they are still being felt. I went because it was the only thing that felt remotely related to what I want to do with my life.

In my defence, I tried to do the trip legitimately. I told Mum I wanted to take a sick day off school for it, but she said I couldn't go in case they found out I was faking illness. So I then decided to write to my music teacher and convince her it would 'contribute to my education by allowing me to see a professional performer live, given that I am going to be a singer'. I also stupidly added that no one as good as PJ Harvey was ever going to play a gig on this godforsaken island. The old hag wrote this really patronising reply about how she couldn't grant me leave because it would set an 'unfair precedent'. These grown-ups are constantly hassling you to work out what you want to do with your life and toe the line, but when you do they tell you that you still can't have what you want. So I had to take the painful option (typical me, typical me, typical me). I bunked off school, having told everyone what I wanted to go that night, thereby ensuring I'd get caught.

I suppose I couldn't have caused more trouble if I'd planned to because I'd told Aunt Carol (the only person I know in London) that Mum had said we could stay with her for the night of the gig. I was taking full advantage of the fact that my mum and Aunt Carol weren't speaking and hoped that Mum would buy the idea I was staying at Jay's that night.

Big mistake, firstly because Mum doesn't like me staying at Jay's anyway. She's always saying how dating a local boy is beneath me, which is classist bollocks. But the second reason it was a big mistake is that Mum is convinced Aunt Carol has been buying stuff from my granddad to stop her getting it when she dies. Mum thinks it's unforgivable, although, having said that, she thinks lots of things are unforgivable.

But anyway, the gig. It felt kind of thrilling, going to the mainland with Jay first thing in the morning. His battered Mini joined the grid of cars on the bottom deck of the car ferry. He was shaking as he drove on the motorway for the first time.

I put the new Smashing Pumpkins record, 'Adore' in the tape deck. Looking at him, as he edged through the traffic, I listened to the words, 'You love him' echo over and over again from the speakers. And I looked at Jay and wondered whether I did. Did I just like the fact that he was helping me to live my life? I could see from the look he gave me that he thought I was relating the words of the song to him.

It was the first time I'd been to London as an adult. I couldn't believe how stylish the women were. On the escalator coming out of Shepherd's Bush Tube, I passed this woman who just transfixed me. She was wearing a black coat with a big fur collar, and her black hair was in a tight bob. She was so enchanting. As I passed her, she caught my eye and smiled and, for a moment, I wondered if she was an older version of me coming back to watch at this key moment of my life. I thought that coat looked like it was made of black feathers, but maybe I imagined that.

Aunt Carol lives in this plush house in Shepherd's Bush, all hanging herbs and bay windows. She wanted to talk about Mum, but I just wanted to get ready for the gig. In a living room full of rare books and art prints I pulled out my clothes, looked at the stuff on the shelves, and wondered if she'd ever actually read these books. Something makes me doubt Aunt Carol ever curls up in front of a log fire with Milan Kundera's The Unbearable Lightness of Being.

I seriously object to people using art an accessory to an experience, rather than just letting it be an experience of itself. I come from a family of philistines!

I finally got to wear the clothes I've wanted to. Silver lipstick to go with a clip in my new, white-blonde bob. I had found this great see-through black top, just like D'Arcy Wretsky wore on the last Smashing Pumpkins tour. Skin-tight black plastic trouser. Very Goth. With his blonde tips and Adidas t-shirt Jay didn't really match but he had got me there. He said, "I don't recognise you," and I replied, "Yeah, that's the idea." The thing is, the only way I can become a new woman is by burning off everything about the little girl.

My heart was thudding when we queued up outside the venue. I couldn't believe how cool the London crowd were. I saw every type of band t-shirt, for bands I'd never heard of. In the queue there were indie boys in their Kappa tops, and

Guardian readers with their horn-rimmed glasses. Then there was this breed of woman like me.

They'd all clearly cut their own hair. They'd assembled outfits that were a bit Courtney Love and a bit PJ Harvey, this tide of feather boa and mink and satin, winding into the venue like a glamorous snake. I was sure I saw Louise from the band Sleeper amongst them.

Inside the venue neither Jay nor I knew what to do. I realised that the whole set up around a gig was incredibly thrilling. Neither of us wanted to admit to each other that we hadn't done this before. I was so glad I had made the effort to dress up or I'd have felt like a right tramp. There were some serious glamour pusses there and, in the toilet, a girl told me she loved my top. In the mirror we all competed for space to add sequins by our eyes. Heartfelt friendships were made over the powder compacts. Women kept complimenting me on how thin I was. On the island my thinness is always source of concern. Never a good thing.

Jay and I hung around the merch stand for ages while the venue filled up with people trying not to spill pints before the show started. I couldn't believe how beautiful the t-shirts and vinyls were, and the fact I couldn't afford any of them made them even more amazing. It seemed impossible to ever think you could make something that beautiful for people to buy, take home, and hold to their hearts. But I felt determined to throw myself at the wall trying. I seemed to think that if I stood by Polly's merch for long enough my career in music would somehow start. That, like her, I could create art that meant something to people, which offered them a new way to live and which made them feel less alone.

But I was silently taking notes. I was learning where to put the merch stand, what time the support act came on, how long they played for, what you played through the speakers before you came onstage, how you came onstage, etc. Knowing all this training would be important when my turn came.

I insisted we got to the front, but it was just impossible. I'd spent too long looking at posters while an arty racket of drums and violins raged on the stage. And now I couldn't get close to the action. Some of those women have sharp elbows and I had to make do with a pretty decent view of it all from a few rows back.

Jay was stunned into silence by it all, and I found myself scanning the stage for the moment Polly would come on. Is that where she'd stand? Was that her set list taped to the floor? Why had she chosen this song to play before she appeared?

I listened to the background music with such intensity. I asked myself questions all the time, questions Jay just wouldn't get. I didn't know how deep I was supposed to sit in the experience. It's an ongoing uncertainty that I am sure sets me apart and makes me genuinely weird. I was determined to soak up every moment of it.

The lights went down and I felt so excited I thought I'd faint. Polly's band filed on stage and, as she followed them a scream went up. I'd thought about this woman so much. Her songs had carried me through so much dead time, and she was just standing right there, not even knowing I existed. With her tiny shoulders, her focused expression, and her hacked-at black curls, she was so dramatic that I just **knew** we were from the same tribe. I just knew that at some point, when my features grew in and my image was in place, I would be raised above the crowd in the same way, with them looking to me. Her neck bones were straining out from above a strappy black top. The earpiece, leading to a small pack on the back hem of her red leather dress looked so professional. What choices did she make to become that creature up there? A slavish cheer went up when she touched the mike. I felt like I could die. It was all too much. There was no outlet.

I was learning, fast. I saw that you had to give the audience the room to want you. No, to **need** you. Jay finished the dregs of his pint as a low acoustic guitar thrum built. The crowd whooped, but Polly didn't react. In a really low, heavy voice she started to sing. "I Think I'm A Mother." Her baritone made her slender femininity seem really strange, and I wondered who started a set with a slow song about an accidental pregnancy. Who comes onstage in such understated clothes, barely moving, barely smiling? And then it hit me. When you're onstage you do what you want to do, what you **need** to do. You make them come with you, no compromises.

It was all pretty dark and heavy. After the first song, Jay asked if I was enjoying it, and I said that I'd never been happier. And I meant it.

Afterwards I was on cloud nine. Jay seemed more bothered about buying a kebab from a London takeaway. He was really into this whole thing about spending a fiver on some meat in pitta bread that you got in a plastic tray. "This," he said, as we scoffed in a grim takeaway near Aunt Carol's, "is what London's all about." It made me wonder if throughout Polly's various journeys into her inner torment he was just dreaming of hot meat. Despite that thought I kissed him on his chilli-stained cheek. "Thank you so much for today," I said. "You really are the best boyfriend."

He smiled as he dabbed his napkin on his lips. He looked like he couldn't believe his luck. "I am, aren't I?" he said, as I went to fetch him a Coke, because Jay likes to have a Coke with his snacks.

I knew that it'd kick off when we returned to Aunt Carol's. I just **knew** it.

When she opened the door, I could see right away from her expression that Mum had called.

"Sorry we're a bit late," I said.

"Not sorry enough," she said, looking me square in the eye.

We squeezed past her and I decided to try and pretend that I hadn't picked up on her body language, even though that never works with people and that night would prove no exception. I reminded myself that if I was to achieve my ambitions people would inevitably get trampled on. Jay started blowing up the bed in the living room in really dramatic puffs, glad to have a job, and Aunt Carol trailed in behind us. "Your mother just called." Her hollow voice suggested she didn't know where to start. "I'd say you're in a bit of trouble, young lady."

Jay looked up, red-faced. "I knew it," he said, hoarse.

Aunt Carol folded her arms and leaned against the doorframe.

29

"What did she say?" I asked, feeling my buzz rapidly fade.

"Tell Emma it isn't worth coming home," she said.

Jay's face paled. He knew this would affect him. Us.

Aunt Carol handed me the phone.

"Honestly, Emma. Just call her. I think she really just wants to hear that you're okay."

"Yeah, right."

She eyeballed me warily. "You do now she carries a t-shirt of yours in her handbag, don't you?"

"Why?"

Her shoulders dropped. "Because it has your smell. Because she misses you when you're not around."

This was news to me. "You expect me to believe that?" I asked. "Nice try."

"Look. I know you fight. But she loves you."

"I'll call her," I said, feeling my shoulders rise. "I'll call and say she's right. It's not worth me coming home."

"No. I know you better than that," Aunt Carol said. "I know you're more considerate than that, Emma."

The thing is, she was right. I had to admit, this gig had put people through a lot of trouble. It wasn't really on.

I took the phone off her.

"I'm sorry, Aunt Carol. I just really needed to go."

*"No. You really **wanted** to."*

I dropped my head. "Yeah, you're right."

She put her hand on my shoulder. "I remember what it was like being your age," she said. "I'm not that bloody old. Make the call."

My heart dropped. There was no getting around it.

I called Mum.

She picked up after one ring.

"Mum, I'm sorry," I said, surprised at how sincere I feel.

No reply.

"Mum? I mean it."

I realised then that I did mean it, as well.

"I really am sorry," I repeated.

When Mum eventually spoke, she was so quiet I could barely hear her.

"You really are a nasty little shit," she said. "It had to be your Aunt Carol, didn't it? You had to force me to call the one person I didn't want to, didn't you?"

The entry ended right there. I exhaled, put the diary down on the floor, folded my legs and closed my eyes. I tried to remember what happened next.

It came to me slowly. Mum and Emma didn't speak to each other for weeks. Mum didn't accept Emma's apology and kept calling her a bitch. Emma insisted that the trip was something she'd just had to do. Whole news stories came and went in the media but in the house nothing changed. Emma was grounded, which forced things to end with Jay, which made Emma hate Mum back. After three weeks of us all eating in separate camps I went into Dad's study and asked him, over his newspaper, "Haven't they spoken yet?"

I remember how he didn't lower the paper, but how when he spoke his tone suggested it was like I was asking about the advancement of two huge, opposing armies.

"Of course not," was his reply.

"Seriously?" I asked.

"Seriously," Dad confirmed without moving.

It scared me the way women could create this kind of atmosphere. Us men were just useless, flapping around with newspapers. We had no shamanic power.

"Do you think Emma will always be like this?" I asked.

"Your mother was when I first married her. So yeah."

He made her sound like a colt he had valiantly tamed. I had never thought of my mum like that.

I closed my eyes tighter and tried to think back to what happened next. I remembered that I didn't leave his study. I felt like I *couldn't* leave until he'd done *something* about the situation.

In the end he realised I wasn't leaving, dropped the newspaper, and narrowed his eyes.

"With mothers and daughters, it's not like it is with you and me, Jeff," he said. "This stuff goes deep." His eyebrows knitted together. "*Really* deep."

31

"It's all about nothing though really, isn't it?" I answered.

The paper went back up. "I wouldn't let them hear you say that," he said.

"You've got to do something, Dad. You're-" I tried to think of a term that might emotionally engage him. "You're the man of the house."

The paper didn't move.

"There's a vacancy for that position. If you're so interested in taking it."

For some reason, on that one day I didn't accept Dad's apathy. "Fine. I will," I said.

I went into the hallway. Mum's Dior handbag was under the telephone table. I could hear her conspiring with some friend on the phone in the kitchen. I felt so angry and frustrated that my fingers were shaking as I opened the clasp. I knew what I was looking for and, as I listened for footsteps, I felt that soft fabric; Emma's Bugs Bunny t-shirt. I knew Mum kept it there, and I knew Emma didn't know that. I pulled it out and leapt up the steps. Emma's door was, of course, locked. I knocked on Jim Morrison's face.

"No," she said, bored.

"It's Jeff."

A stifled sigh, and a moment later the lock slid back. She was wearing a long black t-shirt, her legs and feet bare. "What's up?"

"Let me in for a second."

"Girl trouble?" she said, with what sounded like a hint of a smile. She turned as I followed her inside. Vinyls and t-shirts were spread over the floor. I saw the words 'Bratmobile' and 'Bikini Kill', and felt a bit scared. David Bowie's face seemed to be everywhere. The collages on her wall were so densely packed that you couldn't see the wallpaper. Kate Moss, Marilyn Monroe, James Dean (who I wittily liked to call James Dead). She had her own audience up here and they were so edgy it was little wonder she never left her kingdom for the likes of us.

"Oh, Jeff," she said, turning to face me. "It's not *boy trouble* is it?"

"Shut up."

"Because it's okay if it is and -"

I handed her the t-shirt.

"What's this?"

"Mum keeps it in her handbag. She doesn't want you to know. But she does."

Emma's eyes widened as she looked at the t-shirt.

"I thought that was just something Aunt Carol said."

Her eyes were actually trembling.

"Well, it's not."

I opened the t-shirt. There were mascara marks on it. "See that?" I said, pointing at them. "That's from where she tries so hard to smell you on it that she ruins her makeup."

Emma laughed.

"And we know, don't we, that Mum doesn't let anything unimportant ruin her makeup?"

She considered the t-shirt. Then me.

"Well, every day's a school day."

"So you'll talk to her?"

She started to pull on her pyjama bottoms.

"Fine."

"Now?"

"Yes, Jeff. Now," she said. She considered me, askance. "You're alright."

"I know."

And just like that, it ended.

Chapter Seven

I flicked forward to the next entry. It was marked '09', and I realised it was a year before Emma had returned to her diary.

As I stood up, I wondered if Emma and Mum's relationship actually ever recovered from her trip to London. Or if, in some way, it planted the seeds of what came next.

School is finally over in five days. In five days, I won't have to pretend I have some kind of control over my identity purely because I hike my school skirt higher up than I should.

My band can be like a suit of armour. It can protect me from the world. I can form my own gang of girls, with a name and a logo. Other women can rally under that banner. It's harder to mess with us if we're a bunch. We can create little spaces where other women can find themselves, using art.

I've been thinking about this a lot.

I need women who don't just want to be in a band to attract boys. I need women who are driven enough that they'll push the boundaries of what a band is. I need a bunch of stars, women who insist on saying the truth, women who will have their own following within our audience. They need to be artists within their own right, and I can't be petty about that. I have to encourage them to be the best they can be. I'm sick of other people (especially girls my age) trying to peg each other back because they feel threatened. I am going to go out there and find the right women. I'll dress up, and I'll go to the coolest places and I'll find a way to convince the coolest women there to join me. They'll be waitresses, painters, and Go-Go dancers. If I need to teach some snake-hipped Medusa how to play bass guitar, then I can.

Since the high school gig, things have changed for me at

school. Why couldn't that have happened sooner? As soon as the prison door opens a little bit, the prison doesn't look so bad. Having been sniggered at in the diner, having had people cough the word 'freak' as I pass, I now have girls in the year below stand there with looks of amazement as I pass. Is this what art does? It unlocks something weird in people, and you can't put it back in once it's out.

All my unrequited love affairs have now taken on a new lease of life. You get a bit of confidence and suddenly you're so much more attractive. Take yesterday; a tedious afternoon in the grotty school library where I tried to read Roddy Doyle's 'Paddy Clarke Ha Ha Ha'. I can't, for the life of me, tie up the excited quotes on the back of the book with the dirge that's inside. I want words to cut, to draw blood. In pursuit of that feeling, I'm listening to PJ Harvey's Sheela-Na-Gig on one earphone while I try to work. It's all menstruation, sexual humiliation. It's real art.

And I am just about to embarrassingly write some of her lyrics out when Billy sits down opposite me.

We don't speak. He half-smiles. I can smell him. He raises his eyes at the earphone as if ask what it is I'm listening to.

I see how his dark curls lap over his ears. His hands are all cut, and I remember that he works in his dad's fields in the summer.

*I lean over and offer an earphone. He takes it and, for one thrilling, heart-pulsing minute, we are in the shared space between my ears, listening to this twisted, visceral, blues-y story of a woman pulling open her vagina and laughing hysterically. I don't know if he actually hears any of the words. I am pretty sure he's trying to smell my hair, but for that minute I actually feel close to a boy, far closer than I ever felt to Jay, when he tried to kiss me in the back of his Dad's car. Something occurs to me, that you should let a man into your world on your own terms. And if you're going to do that, then you should probably let **people** into your world on your own terms. And what better way to do that than through your art?*

I exhale. I think, if only she had taken her own advice.

Something seems to burn in my gut. Emma knew, on some level, what was coming. Why else would she have written all that?

And if she knew what was coming, why didn't she avoid it from happening?

Chapter Eight

Tonight the band is supporting Rosary. Their singer, Adam, comes into The Dublin Castle and sits in the corner, and has a pint on his own. He's reading a book. It's called The Torture Garden.

I'm at the other end, trying to write our set list for tonight, but kind of watching him too. I've never met a pop star with a real fan base before.

He's very thin, very pale, has intense dark eyes and the black leather jacket pulled up to his elbow reveals some faint scars on his arm. At one point he smiles at me, but these young girls bothering him break his smile. Some of them want him to sign books-for some reason, Albert Camus' The Outsider. He's patient with them, but I can see from the other side of the room that there's this one girl, whose emaciated legs suggest bulimia, that just won't leave him alone. When he goes to the bar to get another glass of water, she goes over to him with this hunched posture that says, she knows she's taking this too far, but she's just got one more thing to ask. Much as I cringe, watching this, I know how easily I could be one of these girls. I **am** *one of those girls, but something inside me has twisted and made me use that feeling to form a band, to get gigs like this over a phone and find ways to bundle the band into a rehearsal room in London. The alternative would be waiting around in pubs during the day for men like him. And there's enough dead time in life as it is.*

I watch out of the corner of my eye as he takes her into the corner of the bar. I can't hear what he says to her but at the end he gives her a slip of paper. An autograph? She leaves without a sound, contented. As soon as she hits daylight, I hear her scream. The closing door cuts the sound out. He closes his eyes.

I find myself worrying that he'll watch my sound check. I don't know why I care. He's too thin, twitchy, and he looks scared. Do I care because his band is all over the music weeklies? Do I care because I'm shallow? If he says we're crap, how will I handle it?

I'm relieved but also disappointed that during our sound check he doesn't come through the doors to the venue. But we've just finishing the final song when I see him at the back, alone, of course. It's like he's drenched in an invisible scent called alone-it's sort of pathetic. As if he's a graveyard that you're supposed to only enter with reverence. His arms are folded. I bet men like him, brilliant and useless, spend most of their lives in dead spaces like this. The tech guy leans over the desk and says something to him, and a moment later Adam is gone.

I decide not to think about boys and to just focus on getting ready. One of the big challenges at these gigs is trying to make yourself glamorous in the shite toilets. There are never any locks on the cubicles because of smack heads. It's difficult when you are wearing a cut-off white satin dress, the single white stocking all a part of your "Las Vegas Shotgun Wedding" look. I have made myself ready for the stage a good hour before the doors even open, even down to writing Slut on my thigh in red lipstick. I am dismantling England's idea of the feminine, honouring my Riot grrrl tribe (even if I haven't ever met them), and spreading the message. When I leave the loo I almost smash into Adam on the stairs.

*He's even thinner up close, but he **is** handsome in a razor-like way, sharp cheekbones, a bit unhealthy looking. "Sorry," he says, with a soft Scottish accent.*

I smile. No words come.

"Loved your sound check. Some lyrics that are actually… real," he says, as some fat bloke burps past us on the stairwell.

"Th-thanks," I stammer. "I've been reading your lyrics too. They sound…good."

They had so many layers. I kept reading them and thinking, *"look at all these **layers**."*

I feel so, so frustrated by my inane smile and my inarticulacy. All those months spent looking out the window waiting for something to happen, resenting the world for denying you opportunities, and then when destiny crashes into you being rendered mute.

"Well, you know," he says, averting his gaze.

We let someone pass on the stairs, and he starts to look up. I wonder if he's indulging in this moment between us.

"It's not really how I want it to be, though," he says. "It's become all about making hits, and not about what we're trying to say."

"Yeah. I know the feeling," I answer.

I don't.

As we talk, he looks very deeply into my eyes. It feels like we're having a Deep Meaningful Conversation, but so little is actually being said. That's how men like him get success, I think. They know how to look into your eyes, and touch your soul, and switching that ability on is the difference between having a bit of record company interest or having a big fat recording contract and then getting to break little girls' hearts.

"Look, we've got a few hours before the gig," he says. "Fancy getting out of here, having a pint at The Good Mixer?"

I try to play it cool and fail. I nod enthusiastically and forever.

The girls snarl at me as we pass by them and out into the white gold autumn sun of the late afternoon. I laugh and put on my heart-shaped sunglasses and let the late afternoon London sun pour over me. I feel all London Bridge and long indulgent afternoons at The Tate. London is this big beautiful dragon curling its tail around me. A new way of living has opened up and I'm folding myself into it. As we walk down the street, Eddie Izzard, with a Prada handbag at his elbow waves his hand. "Afternoon, Adam," he says.

Adam waves back, uninterested. Oh, to be famous enough to be uninterested.

I expect The Good Mixer to be full of people like Morrissey,

39

Alex James, or at least for Keith Allen to be there having a game of cards. But it's not like that. It's full of black labradors, and people with overgrown facial hair and piercings. People sneer or dismiss us. Given my outfit, they probably think we've just got married. What would our wedding be like?

As we wait at the bar, any ideas I had that walking in with a pop star would allow me to enter a hallowed space are dismissed. There are no 'pop stars' here. At best, Adam is just about odd enough to be allowed in.

As we sit under the gilt windows and watch a game of pool, he drinks a bottle of Bud. And I enjoy the mild gender subversion of being the one sipping a pint. He settles, and I tell myself that as a feminist I mustn't suck up to him.

"I caught some of the lyrics to that last song," he said.

"What did you think?"

He sips. "We've been singing about similar things. There's lots of body horror in my lyrics, self-harming, bulimia, masturbation. I get so tired of people being portrayed as though they're polished." He watches as a man, his beer gut drooping from his Kappa t-shirt, lurches past us. "I just see people as walking ruins, physical, psychological ruins, lurching towards you like a car crash."

I feel like every part of my body is working at hyper speed. I know I'll feel exhausted after speaking with him. I haven't had conversations like this before, even if Charlotte, Saskia and I have fantasised enough about this kind of thing for me to almost feel prepared. One or two boys in my Media Studies seminars talked a bit like this, and I did wonder what it'd be like if someone I fancied had this kind of chat. Would I actually get to talk about something interesting? Could I actually start to work one or two things out? I used to dismiss those men. But, on another level, I am dying for this conversation and have lots to say. I want to talk until I drop. I feel pregnant with the future.

So what I do is say nothing.

His expression suggests he has interpreted my silence as wisdom. These men always get us talking, thinking we have these feminine, beautiful inner worlds that are totally sealed, but they don't realise we just want to be involved in it all and that we're too smart to think we've got it all worked out like men do.

"What do you think?" he asks.

I draw breath.

"It strikes me as a bit odd that when a man sings about women's bodies he gets critical praise for discussing it, but when a woman like Courtney Love does it she gets portrayed as out of control, hysterical."

He smiles and sucks his top lip of foam. "What about Polly Harvey?" he asks.

"She's spreading the feminist message in music like the Riot grrrls are, were, in the US. Just like I'm about to."

He nods, impressed. "I love PJ Harvey."

It's almost like he **knows** about me listening to her while I counted the days to leave school. He talks like he knows her personally. He probably does.

Adam and Polly, having a drink. And then, a few days later, Adam and Emma having a date. Sitting in a tree.

"But look at Princess Diana," I say, swilling my glass. "The tabloids treated her like a pariah and then all mourned her dying as if their own mother had died."

"True," he says. "To me, Diana was a true rock star, throwing herself downstairs and all that. That's proper Keith Moon stuff."

I laugh. "That's pretty dark."

It's worse than that, I think. It shows a sick mind.

"It is what it is," he says, sipping his beer.

It's hard to disagree with that statement.

"So why do you write about that stuff?" I ask.

"Because it's real. I have to find a way to keep it all in the 'real', even if it's depressing." He looks right at me.

I decide that men like him can look right through you, at every layer. It's an act of restraint for them to not comment on all they've seen inside you. "I went to see a performance of Sarah Kane's Blasted the other night," he continues. "It's all rape, incest. Everything to do with the play is a means to just channel something brutally real at the audience throughout

41

the whole performance. "

I read some of her in the library. "You don't think she overdoes it?"

He shakes his head. "Even if she does, it's only trying to rebalance the lack of attention these matters normally get in the media. What she's doing is still worthwhile."

I decide that bracing honesty is the only way to keep someone like this interested. I am officially about to get started. I have rehearsed telling this kind of stuff to Melody Maker. But he'll do.

"Well, the reason I talk about bad sex so much in my songs is that I don't know any other kind. I like how Courtney and Polly sing about it as frightening, physically painful. All the emotions that come with it are scary, obsessive, terrifying. I'm, we're, tired of sex only being sung about by men," I say, proud of my boldness. I can feel it. Tonight is going to be an important night. When things **finally start to change**.

"I agree," he says, with an admiring smile. "And I find it scary too. Didn't even lose my virginity until I was twenty-one."

Emboldened, I decide to go for the jugular. "So two rock stars having a pint. People would expect us to end up in some cheap hotel room tonight, having awkward sex, before the real way we handle intimacy outside theoretical conversations is revealed."

I know saying this is a risk, but he smiles even wider. I decide he likes this postmodern, meta-conversation about what is happening. I tell myself not to slide into irony. So many fatal mistakes, just waiting to happen. Waiting like men in dark suits behind the door.

"Yeah. I spend hours convincing you I'm not like other men. Then after some crap sex I fall asleep. The next day I promise to call and don't. You feel really hurt because of the betrayal."

"And I become a psycho bitch, turning up at your hotel, getting the worst of both worlds as your fans then hate me too."

"And then you see this conversation as a new layer of male deception you now need to be familiar with, when even

42

apparent candour is just another form of cunning."

"And we both walk away a little more hurt and bruised into our next relationship."

I know 'relationship' is a risky word to use during a first drink. But it glances over him, and he drains his bottle. It is quite a sight to behold and watching the hunger with which he drinks I wonder why he doesn't have a beer belly. It's like he's trying to suck something from the bottom of the bottle. I know this is not a good sign. But then again, he is the type of man to read a book in a pub. Perhaps this is just what rock stars do.

"Or we could subvert the whole thing and treat each other kindly and respectfully," I suggest.

He looks over my shoulder. "It'd be hypocritical of me to promise that, knowing how pathetic I am. As a man."

He clocks my reaction.

"I can only disappoint you," he says.

I exhale and decide that I like that excerpt. Simply because he hasn't disappointed her, or what Mum describes as 'led her astray' yet. **Yet** being the key word here. Not only is Emma still alive but also at this point I really believe there is any choice of outcomes. It's that simple, and that frustrating. Adam could have handled what was to come next in so many ways. In so many better ways. At this moment in her story I can see the lights of the train approaching, but the collision is still a good way off.

Emma is with me, in the annexe. I am learning from her how a man is supposed to treat a woman, how you handle your feelings for another person, which the world tells you that you must keep to yourself, which you can't. Something about the way she is speaking to Adam is telling me how I could speak to Ruth, if the chance ever came for us to speak properly. I'm learning how you can have a meta-conversation about your relationship with someone as you get to know them, how you can comment on what you're doing as a part of the way you're relating to someone. These little devices, which make it less exposing telling someone how you feel, while still doing something about it.

*During the gig it's impossible to tell if Adam is in the crowd. But the thought of him being there, the thought that I can force his presence with an exciting enough performance, drives me. I know I have an audience who will see me transform. Finally, it is **my turn**.*

The rhythm section who, for so long, have been a clique that shut me out, click into place as I step up. Their bitchy tendency to close ranks which, for so long, felt like an affront to my leadership, now means that at my most erratic there is a solid base to the music. This means that in the more emotional moments of my performance-when I spin into the audience to crowd surf, or when I kneel on the floor and holler each word like it's my last, are well supported. I have a strong backdrop, which is what any star needs.

I am a star. It strikes me that all you need is for your hair to fall the right way, or for you to hold your shoulders a certain way, and you become Marilyn, Diana, Ava. I deserve kid gloves and treats on trays. I strike poses I've practiced in mirrors, knowing silent girls beneath me will soon copy them. I can see in their eyes that they are taking notes. All the white heat I cultivated in arguments with Mum becomes awesome solar power that I use to charge whole crowds. I'm like Mum now, I have dark power, and men fear my reactions while women fear what I might do next. All those awful situations with her have become tools I can use to dismantle people with, before putting them back together how I want. What seemed like pointless feminine angst was in fact the hard-earned experience of battle, each bloody scrap giving me future advantage. I can almost feel the energy pouring out of my hands and am spoilt for choice with all the ways I can use it. But I know how to use it, to inspire other women, to make it clear that they don't need to be ignored just because they're made to feel like that's 'the way it is'. It is taking everything I have, and I am so frightened I'm shaking, but I am going to show them that is not 'the way it is'.

As the set develops, the placid attention of the crowd becomes a sea of nodding heads, and then little mosh pits break these waves. Women raise their hands above their heads and enjoy sanctioned insanity for a couple of moments. I realise that I can induce in them behaviour that might be cathartic. Riding the wave of this thought, in The Sculptress, I decide to kneel on the stage and scream every single word. Given my outfit, this makes me look like I am having one long honeymoon tantrum, which I quite like. We have never practiced me doing this and I know the music probably won't sustain around that, but tonight I just have to throw myself into infinity.

I am also hoarse by the third line but in an almost military fashion the crowd, mostly women at the front, start waving with two hands in time to the shamanic rhythm of my barks. I am proud of my raw throat, proud of my hollering, proud of the way that in my pretty bridal gown I twirl like a ballerina in a music box. I am like all the female stuff they feared in one twisted bundle that they all want to fuck and kill. I love being that and I love them hating me for it. But for once they can't stop me because I'm protected up here now. I am **the performer**.

I don't look at my band mates, but I feel their shock and pride as I transform in front of them. It is at the end, in a brief skirmish of sound, that I wheel around and see Adam by the mixing desk. I make a mental note, amongst the chaos, to enjoy later. I record that his expression is admiring and that he is scared of me. **At last, men are scared of me**. *All I've ever wanted is to be frightening enough to get noticed.*

His band are, of course, on last. Four skinny men in black jeans playing angular rock. Not quite handsome, but not quite odd enough to be repellent. They have practiced too much. Their singer screams political slogans (I hear, "Abort the royal offspring" and "urban holocaust"). Adam thrashes away on a guitar, stage left. With his shiny gold shirt, unbuttoned, and with his hairspray-drenched mop of dark hair he looks sensational. They have something I don't have, and probably never will. The songs sound like they already existed when strictly speaking they are trying to sell them to us. But they do it with such dismissiveness that the songs seem to have lives of their own that they are merely paying lip service to. And the songs are performed as if they are totalising, justifying entities. You find yourself thinking that these songs could change anything. There is something about them which makes them impossible to ignore and that is frightening because you realise the sense of possibility that music has.

The girls below just scream up at him, and Adam's Mick Ronson face says, "This is all just good fun," and furthermore, "this is what always happens." The songs are slick, efficient, and between-song sips of beer purposefully betray that this is one gig of many. The band's general attitude is, "We aren't going to exhaust ourselves for a hundred people." At the end of the set they all spin around as the outro builds and then the drummer destroys the kit. To ear-splitting feedback, Adam goes over to the singers abandoned pint, picks it up and drains it. People roar as the gold liquid floods down his white cheeks. He smashes the glass on the floor, steps awkwardly over the mess, and leaves the stage.

I notice that his foot is bleeding.

Afterwards, I feel like a soaked sponge of female fluids, sweat, running foundation, vaginal secretion, dried tears. When I queue at the bar for a pint, I am hoping that my leopard print fur covers all the grim realities that are happening under my dress. I can't believe how much work it is dragging around a woman's body with you. All the washing and eating and drinking and then more washing and all of it oozing out of you all the bloody time, betraying you, giving you away.

Adam appears out of nowhere, all popping neck veins and shaving rashes. "You're a fucking genius," he says. One bashful, girlish smile later the fate of the evening is sealed.

I tell him I have missed the last train, and he is smart or disinterested enough to buy the ploy. It is a trick Charlotte taught me; get close to a man you like, literally just hang around them, and even if they don't fancy you, they'll spend the night with you. If you say you've missed your last train, they then have to feel responsible for you. I have found it a useful tactic to spend time with men who otherwise would feel okay abandoning me. You need to have enough proximity to them, Dearest Reader, that it is their responsibility to offer you a bed for the night. But the ploy is quite good as well because men don't want to look like predators and come onto you, which puts you fully in control. If you later decide a chaste sleep on the couch is what you want to do, they give themselves brownie points for allowing that. If you show them a little love, then sex seems very natural, given your situation.

His flat is off Tottenham Court Road. I get the impression the label is paying for it; he talks about it like it is an unwanted child. The Tube ride is a succession of knowing glances between us, given whatever weirdo is making a scene in the carriage. The walk to his house sees a fragile social contract being drawn up. The gap between romance and special friendship is narrow but the membrane between them is strong. I can't make it too easy for him.

In a stark kitchen he offers to make me a cup of tea. It is dark outside as I sit in the bay window of his ruined living room and watch the traffic pass beneath us. He makes me weak Peppermint tea. It occurs to me this is the sort of man who wears shit shoes, who makes weak tea, and I am fully aware of the implications this will have on his morals. But at least the sex with a man like this won't hurt much. He has zero appetite, except to quench his loneliness.

He has placed himself outside of disappointment and, if anything, that has placed me in the role of someone intended to drag him into a sense that he is worthwhile. It's so clever, and so shitty. Adam has cheated the rules of gender. It is women who are supposed to create forcefields around themselves and make people torture themselves second guessing what to do next. But he has kept his male curtness while also appropriating female wiles. Looking out at the London night I think how this is all a neat trick on his part, to ensure he can be utterly selfish and force the woman to be at the same time a mother, a virgin and a whore. I have not yet decided what to do with these options, if anything.

He shows me his lyric booklet as he plays David Bowie's Low on his turntable. I am more entranced than I want to let on. These lyrics have been published in inlay cards for CDs bought around the world. There is a picture of Marilyn

Monroe on the cover. "It was defaced by paint," he says. "She ruined the pictures so they couldn't be used. It reminded me of how Steve from Def Leppard bought a meat cleaver and threatened to cut his hands off so he couldn't play. We spend our lives cultivating skills just to be hamstrung by them if they come to define us."

"She had so much power," I say, touching the pictures with reverence. I know that the next sentence he needs to say, after tonight, is "so do you". The fact that he doesn't say it speaks volumes. I know that he is scared of what I can do, and that if I can somehow grapple control over him then I can do that over any man, and then I can do anything.

*I know that in his remark there is a warped logic at play. But I still retain the possibility that this is how rock stars think; that I still just need to **get** that.*

Besides, I find his idea romantic, the idea that talent is such an albatross that it has to be slain. I envy and crave this frame of mind. Unlike him, I am still at the point where my talent is yet to be agreed upon. I know, in my heart, that it is deeply indulgent to neglect and torture your talent once people have seen it. All I know is that I want to get to the point where I can talk about these things in relation to myself, and not in the abstract. I am a developing photograph. I am doing all I can to develop faster, but he has the confidence of someone who can transform me in a few moments. If he wants to.

How many people have the chance to do that and don't take it?

*As I am trying to come to terms with all the mutilation and starvation in his poetry, he brings me a red pen and asks me to write something in his notebook. Looking out at the filthy, starlit evening I smile, because I am aware that this means he has assigned this as **one of those** evenings. Where a symbolic souvenir is needed, because tonight will be so memorable.*

I love being at the age where you know you are making these little dents on the future. So many other exchanges between people seem weightless.

I am smart enough to be candid; mean spiritedness will cut no ice here. I write a few lines from an Emily Dickinson poem.

I'm Nobody! Who are you? Are you – Nobody - too?

He doesn't smile. He is serious. "Now autograph it," he says.

His choice of words is telling. I can imagine him saying to people that Emma from Cherub wrote this. I'm Emma from Cherub, I say to myself. If my band was called Buggerlugs, would I even be here?

"Hell or high water, Emma," I write.

"I guess we'll soon find out if you mean that," he says.

"What do you mean?"

He stretches, and some script that he's privately played out many times seems to spool across his eyes. Will he let me read it?

I decide not to give into the classic female strategies to get him to open up. There will be no bad sex during this shotgun wedding. I can't bear for that to be what snaps this fragile sense of union. Knowing that he is grasping for the closest failure he can pin disappointing me to. Unlike him, I can tolerate the ambiguity. You see, I am two steps ahead. I have been left my whole life. So being left a little longer works well for me.

We lie next to each other, the boundary between us respected by him with more diligence than I would have ideally liked. I am a bride whose new husband is a eunuch. Why won't he kiss me? If he's not going to kiss me, then what the hell is this?

I am conscious of the perfume I am leaving on his sheets, and conscious that he is conscious of it. I sleep like a girl-foetus in my dress, but I am aware of my attractiveness, the visceral pull of a girl curled at his side. I am aware of my tractor beam, drawing his waist to mine. As I try to sleep, I think of his force field. It is confused, damaged.

My sleep is light and full of bizarre, hot dreams which he's in. I have a dream in which we are about to have sex but when he lies down, he is a woman, and then he is Jay. I have a dream that his penis is a spike and I tell him I can't take it even though I'm really horny, but he insists that I must. I wake up, feeling very wet. In my mental frenzy I decide he is

49

dangling the idea that he is not attracted to me, to coax out my insecurity or pride and get me to come onto him so then he'll have the upper hand.

Then the morning comes, faint and eggshell blue and painfully over-exposed. I become aware of the dust in the corners of his room, of the Polaroids of women on his dressing table in stages of undress, of the sadomasochistic books on his shelf. This man really does not have a healthy mind, I think, as I watch his eyelids flutter. I have kicked off the dress at some point in the night, and I pull it around me like a shamed barmaid in a Western. I can smell traces of vodka on his breath. I have mental images of him masturbating over things that make him feel ashamed, and then the next day doing it all again.

I go to the window, feeling dirty. The city seems to clench. I think of all the hangovers, all the guilt, all the throbbing emotional pain out there. It is like a mirage, and I think how one really strong blast of sunshine could dissolve it all.

In his bathroom, the mug sticks to the stained ochre sink and my reflection is admiring and frightened. I am a dirty girl, kohl-eyed, sallow, dressed in smudged white, a fallen angel clutching her shroud, with wild hair framing her face.

I go downstairs. A back door to a yard is open, a sideways rectangle of startling white light. I walk towards the light, towards the strains of Nirvana Unplugged, playing on a stereo he has placed out there. He is thumbing along with an acoustic guitar. Even in the morning his pose, his cheekbones, it is all magazine worthy. The cigarettes in the ashtrays are bent, the cellos and steel strings. The song Oh Me starts and he hands the guitar across with a mocking smile. It is as if he is asking me to join him in this world, knowing that I don't have what it takes. I wince up at the sun as he leans back in a deckchair and inhales, eyes focusing on me. As I place the guitar on my lap, he hands me a mug of black coffee. I sip it and close my eyes. The sunlight is cleansing. The music will guide me, if I let it in.

What he doesn't realise is that I learned the whole album when I was teaching myself to play guitar, and not just the notes, but all the nuances too. I learnt how to express myself as a guitar player with that record, but I never tried to sing like Kurt. As I sing About A Girl, I make the song sound totally different. I don't need to learn from men, or defer to them, it is time they learn from me. I have spent so long playing the chords on my own, finding my way into the closed envelope of energy that is that song, that I feel like someone is watching me read out my diary.

I think of the cobwebs around the windows inside, the stained sink and the dirty Polaroids. I wonder what it would be like to spend a lifetime among ruined porches littered with cigarette stubs in a vat of morning sun. As my hands run up and down the fretboard, his eyes widen. I perform. I fluff some notes, but it can't be disputed that I have heart.

For once he is speechless. I smile and hand the guitar back to him.

This is the closest the experience will get to nourishing me. I know that in refusing toast and in refusing to ask about him I am jeopardising whatever this is, but I am exhausted, proud, ashamed and sexually frustrated. I just want to go home, get a wrap on the way, have a shower, masturbate and sleep. I'll touch myself thinking about a bloke who's the opposite of him, but then I'll probably have to think about him at the crucial moment.

He walks me to the Tube. When he asks for my number, I write it in eyeliner on a flier. He writes his with a heart around it, and hands it back to me. I don't smile. I just don't give a fuck anymore.

It is strange to think of my sister in this kind of romantic setting. On her return from that trip, Emma did seem more confident. Maybe, in fairness, Adam coaxed something out of her that night and it led to her getting her first review in Melody Maker.

So that was the moment when the idea of living in London became central to her. I never knew what she was thinking. Women were another species. But, for the first time, thanks to this diary, my sister was making me feel a little less intimidated by them.

Chapter Nine

The next morning, I went downstairs to find River lying on his back on the wet lawn. He rolled in my direction as I walked outside. His fringe was obscuring his eyes. It was almost as if he sometimes used it as an organic eye mask.

"What are we doing today?" I asked.

"We're going to make sweet music," he said, squinting at the sun overhead.

As River and I settled down on the balcony outside his bedroom, I felt the hole in me about Emma start to open up. I decided that only Ruth could help me close it, and that I would need to hide my sense of relief about her arrival from River. So when she came onto the balcony that evening, as the sun began to set, I felt good, as if my immature little life had been blessed with a feminine presence that validated it. River and I had pulled some blankets and a stereo out there, along with a few pillows. He was playing Nirvana's In Bloom. Something about Kurt's lyrics gave me this watery, summery feeling that made me think the past could be washed clean, that everything could be renewed. Perhaps I really could live in a world of summer balconies, chlorine and acoustic guitars and perhaps I would never have to leave. It never occurred to me that you could do exactly that. All you had to do was decide that was how your life was.

"Is that marijuana?" she asked, as she looked at River rolling a spliff. She said the word like this was the start of an unusual Biology lesson at school. The curtain of her hanging hair caught the sun that was setting over my shoulder, orange and red. The effect of the music was enhanced by the sound of rustling leaves. In my mind, summer lives in that moment.

"Uh huh," River said.

She stepped amongst the cushions with excessive caution. She was like a cartoon cat burglar entering a house. "Mind if I join? You know how I love hanging out with *the kids*."

"We're not listening to The Beautiful South or Sixpence None The Richer, before you ask," River said.

"Please," she said, making herself comfortable next to me. "I don't just listen to that stuff, River, and you know it."

"Do you like Nirvana?" I asked.

Emma had taught me that this question was the acid test by which to decide if someone was worth bothering with in your life. If they thought, like my mum, that Kurt's singing sounded like someone being sick, it was probably worth cutting your losses there and then. As Emma used to say, "Nirvana are our Beatles."

"Of course," Ruth said. "I'm not stupid. Though he does sound like he's in a lot of pain."

I decided that she'd scraped through the test.

She'd gone red. River passed me the joint. I took a really deep drag, hoping to develop my good mood. I let the sense of lightness carry me, as I felt the top of my head lift. The sensation didn't erase everything bad in my mind, but it did make it all seem a bit further away. Those feelings are like a wound, I thought. It's my pet wound. I can forget it for a bit, but it always gapes open again, yawning out blood.

I realised the other two were looking at me in shock. I could tell neither of them had ever used drugs or alcohol to numb themselves. To them it was just a cool thing to do. But at that moment I was the link between Emma, a dead rock star, and Ruth, the little girl whose eyes had become as big as dinner plates whenever she was near my sister.

Ruth didn't say anything, but she didn't look too pleased about my long drag. Emma at one point had taught me that taking drugs impressed people. If you were the person who'd go further than others it gave you status. I decided it was one lesson of hers that I needed to unlearn.

Emma smoked weed with her friends so often it had made me think it was no big deal. It never seemed to have an effect on her, so I don't even know why she did it. It was only when I

53

mentioned it to my friends, or when I offered some to them, that I saw what it signified. I'd spent so long chatting to Emma while she rolled a spliff that I had thought it a regular part of her life, like when she straightened her hair before a date. But I soon realised that what happened with my older sister, and her female friends, was pretty scary to people my age.

I'd learnt to use this knowledge to my advantage, to skilfully lay out a Rizla and scatter weed generously through it, emphasising how it was nothing to me. I'd seen that it made Emma look edgy. The way she left a bulb at the front was almost artful. For all River's posturing, I could now see he had a false nonchalance about drugs, which Ruth wasn't buying.

As I kept drawing on the joint, I thought of evenings in the garden of our house, a stone's throw away from here. Emma and Charlotte and Saskia would dip their feet in the small pond at the bottom of our garden, smoke and share a bottle of whiskey. From my bedroom I could hear their laughter, and the indiscreet giggles that every now and then turned hysterical. Pressing against my window, I'd realise they were talking about sex. Emma would even call me over and ruffle my hair. I once glowed inside when I heard Charlotte use word 'cute'. But whenever I tried to get Charlotte into a conversation they'd hold back and look to Emma for advice on if they could really talk to me. And Emma would pretend not to have seen those looks and just focus on her joint. As I smoked on that balcony, I mimicked her technique, the generous clasp of her fingers, as if nicotine stains were something to aspire for.

When I offered the joint to Ruth it seemed to take a long time for her to take it. I leant back on the blanket and looked up at the sky. Long, thin clouds were lined with red. Ruth laid the spliff on an ashtray, went to her room, and came back with some CDs.

River leafed through them. "The Great Escape, Mosley Shoals, and The Fugees. Not bad."

Ruth narrowed her eyes and looked out at the garden. "I'm so glad my artistic tastes meet with your approval," she said.

"The Great Escape is Blur's shittest album, though," he

added. "The sense of vaudeville is taken to ridiculous extremes. It lacks the visceral quality of Parklife."

"It's *vaudeville*," Ruth replied, pronouncing it differently.

River changed the CD. Oasis' Some Might Say came on.

I felt like I was slipping inside the song. This fresh, sensational, exciting feeling. It was like a rocket taking off. The world seemed to unhinge. River re-lit the joint and put his feet through the gaps in the balustrade. I picked up the guitar and started picking.

"I didn't know you could play guitar, Jeff," Ruth said.

"He can't," River said. "He's learning."

I looked between them.

"Yeah," I said. "I've got some words written. Be good to use them for something. But I can't stand the thought of writing poetry."

"Not all poetry is bad, Jeff," she said, tucking her legs up under her knees.

"Oh yeah?" River said. "Who's worth bothering with? Kurt Cobain was a poet. Jim Morrison was a poet. But who can compete with them?"

Ruth looked at him with eyes so level I wondered if she was trying to control her temper. "Sylvia Plath, Phillip Larkin…"

"And what did Phillip Larkin do?" River interrupted.

"Well, he was a librarian…"

River snorted. "Yeah, and how sexy is that?" he said.

"Well, he had this really complex love life, with two women at the same time," Ruth explained, with the patience of a teacher.

River looked at the setting sun, with an expression that suggested boredom as much as wonder. "I don't think a librarian is going to have the same insight into human nature as Jim Morrison," he said.

"Why? Do you think wearing leather trousers somehow makes you wiser?"

River's mouth opened but nothing came out. I wondered how often Ruth said something that he didn't have a comeback for.

"We're going to turn his words into songs," River said. This

55

was news to me. "Drums, bass, guitars. We'll record the lot." He looked over his shoulder at me as he puffed smoke through his fringe. "Ruth plays piano really well. And violin," he said, with grave seriousness. "You could add some bits if you want, Ruth."

Ruth stood up. "That's a magnificent offer, River. But no, you're alright. You don't need my *bits*."

It seemed to me a warning shot from the adult world. A suggestion that whatever River and I did would not come to anything. So what did Ruth think *would* be a good use of my time?

River leaned over to me. "Probably for the best," he said. "She'd only add a load of harpsichords and make it sound like something out of the court of Louis IV."

Ruth rubbed down her sweater, as if there was ash on it. "Well, this has been illuminating. I'm off to read some overrated poetry on the lawn, like the pretentious fop that I am," she said.

"Ruth's intimated by my sheer raw talent," River said, as she stepped over him. Blowing a plume of smoke above his head.

Chapter Ten

That night, as River and I tried to set basslines to my wobbly guitar riffs, I could hear the strains of Nina Simone from Ruth's room next door. I fretted that Ruth might come in and say she was being driven to distraction by our musical meanderings, or something equally cutting that would make me give up on music altogether. I realised I was having a lot of imaginary conversations with her in my head. But she didn't come in and say anything, and my fear of the diary, and the silence of the annexe, began to fade. I started to put together a plan to ensure I wouldn't have to see this night through alone.

As River practiced, I took cushions from this sofa on the landing, and some blankets. I created two makeshift beds on the balcony and saw that the sky had turned to a deep violet. As the crickets on the lawn grew quieter, our voices reduced to a whisper. We went from lying down with our instruments, to closing our eyes, to slipping under a thin veil of sleep.

When I woke up, the sunlight was a painful, white experience. The sky was pure and blue. I stood up. The blades of glass below us were illuminated by drops of dew. The slanting sun lit rows of it into diamonds column. The world felt clean and fresh. I tried to forget about *the wound*.

I stepped over a battered acoustic guitar and a full ashtray and went downstairs. The door to the garden was open and, as I went through it, Ruth was facing me, sat at the garden table. She was leafing through a novel from under a sunhat, with a carafe of fresh coffee sat next to her. It struck me that she was probably living the life of a character in some French novel I didn't know about. The faint plume of coffee steam was mixing with the mist over the lawn. As I neared, I noticed a plate of croissants and pastries.

"Freshen up, then come and join me," she said. "I made up a new toiletry bag in the bathroom."

I helped myself to one of River's clean t-shirts and boxers, and then spruced up in the bathroom. By the time I got downstairs, Ruth had placed her book face down on the table. I picked up a warm croissant, tore off a strip, and smeared it with butter. As I reinvigorated myself with the coffee, I felt Ruth study me. With the freshly cut grass still holding buds of dew, the morning felt glorious. Ruth turned her face up to the sun.

"So you'd rather be here than with your parents?"

"I guess so."

"I wonder why," she said, as if it were a point of academic interest.

As I heard music playing from her bedroom I revelled in the warmth of her attention. I gradually recognised the song, The Undertones' Teenage Kicks, as one I had associated with my first crush. The fact that it was playing at the first moment Ruth and I were alone together felt like a powerful message that I was too dumb to understand.

"I don't know," I finally said, taking a glossy Danish pastry.

"A shrink might say you wanted to return to a familiar childhood haunt."

"I don't look at your house as a haunt," I said.

"But it was. There were times when we couldn't get you out of here." She closed her eyes. "Not that you weren't always welcome, Jeff."

"Here I can do what I want, at least."

She screwed up her nose. I noticed a row of new freckles on them.

"I don't think our parents are so different, you know," she said. "Do you see them buying croissants?" She stirred her coffee. "*I'm* basically River's parent. I have everything but the stretch marks."

I had this weird sense she wanted to say, "Like Emma was your parent." There was this whole other conversation going on that wasn't being put into words, something to do with the music and the blades of grass. But Ruth didn't say that, and I wasn't sure where the thought had come from.

"Did you want more from this summer then?" I asked.

"It's not that, though they do think of me as someone that's obsessed with my A Levels. I know River just thinks of me as a swot."

"I don't see you that way."

She smiled and looked down. "I know you don't, Jeff," she said. The smile faded. "And yeah, I want to give myself a decent start at life. But just because I'm smart enough to not steal from the local newsagent doesn't mean there isn't more to me than studying."

She grimaced and poured herself coffee. I watched the crème swirl on the surface as she sipped at the dark liquid.

"There's more to life than books you know," I said. "But not much more."

"Yeah, I know the quote. So what's the 'not much more'? Writing?"

Somehow she knew how important the writing was, I decided.

"Maybe."

"Well if you ever need a second opinion on your scribblings, I'll be playing wet nurse all summer to his dibs. Speaking of which..."

River had appeared in the doorway, a newspaper under his arm. "Christ," he said, looking at us. "What a couple of wet flannels. Have you decided which of you is the biggest victim?"

"I see you've finished your paper round then," Ruth said.

"I need a coffee, a bacon sandwich, and a shit," he announced, in reply.

"Not too bad," Ruth replied. "But it might cloud over later."

River put a Pain Au Chocolat in his mouth and threw the newspaper on the table. Between the colour supplements a porn mag fell out. Knave.

"I see you've been doing your old trick of putting porn in a newspaper before your deliveries and then walking out," I said.

"Of course," River answered. "It *is* a Sunday."

"He's showing off, for you," Ruth said.

"She's showing off, for you," River said, wiping crumbs from his mouth.

"I remember the time the newsagent came outside and made you empty the newspaper on the pavement. And you tried to front him out by making out the porno had somehow slipped in there."

"Vintage edition," River said, not listening. "Reader's Wives. The letters pages are pure fiction from start to finish."

"I'm just *so* shocked," Ruth said. "It's not like I have my own vagina or anything."

River and I put up a dilapidated set of goalposts and played football while Ruth read on the terrace. I wondered how pretentious my earlier remarks now seemed given my adolescent keenness to kick a ball around for hours. We started practicing. I thought of the afternoons Emma and her band had practiced in the boathouse, and how the vortex of sound they had created had seemed impossibly evocative, a feeling enhanced by knowing it was a sound completely made by *girls*. I wished I had a song rich enough to lose myself in. But there were just chords I couldn't quite play, and melodies that remained out of reach. When it seemed as if we didn't have any more ideas River said, "There's a beach party by Whitecliff Bay tonight. A few of us are going to camp on the beach. Bonfires, spliffs, impressionable young things. I'll save you space in my tent."

I thought of arriving at a beach with my belongings on my back, knowing I would be spending a night on the sand. I wasn't sure if I would feel free, or as if it would mean I'd never been more lost.

The thought of being around all those people made me realise I needed some time alone in the annexe, with Emma.

Chapter Eleven

When you're brought up in the backwoods, the city has this massive sense of glamour. When you arrive in London, there's such potency to it. It's in the vibrant colours of the posters, pasted one on top of the other, a stack of events you feel you can't miss, and the faces that streak past you, as you try and follow a map to your new digs. The faces all have etched in them a truth you find terrifying but that you can't articulate.

People's expressions speak of naivety followed by heartache. A carousel of emotions experienced often enough to permanently re-arrange the features. And you sense, as well, in the lascivious glances of the men, and in the disinterested gaze of the vendors, that behind all this London has a huge wrecking ball that will eventually destroy everyone. Its presence looms in the layered smells of grilled meat, on top of the scent of cigarettes, on top of the scent of doorway piss. London whispers in your ear, at every moment, "You'd better have an exit plan, or you are getting fucked."

But I don't have a plan. Adam is a mere phone number on a scrap of paper and, if I ring him, he could just not pick up. A friend of a friend has helped me get a flat near Goldsmiths, using a loan from Dad. When I eventually get there, sweating and tired, London's great unveiling begins.

My flatmates are striking in their unworldliness, and even I can see that. In my Baby doll dress with Peter Pan collar and my shiny Mary Janes I bring with me the meagre confidence I got from my band's support slots at The Wedgewood Rooms. Everyone here is exaggerating the minor contrasts in their backgrounds, making a statement about who we are. But in reality, we are all just walking projections looking for a screen.

Clare is pale, spotty, dowdy and kind. She makes weak tea and stresses over the stains on the kitchen floor that we didn't make. Marie has piercings and a snarl but lacks the flipside warmth I'd expected to find under that hard surface. Neither of them enquires about the guitar I brought, and I have carried it with such prominence that I am disappointed. Why do I think I'm special enough to warrant questions?

Clare is concerned with keeping up regular phone calls to her boyfriend back home. She won't stop talking about him, but he sounds to me like a useless, pretentious boy. Marie keeps talking about 'gender plasticity' and how one person asked her if she was a lesbian and what an outrage this was. They both seem to exist for weekly exhibitions and panel discussions that go nowhere. I go along to these events, having heard that they are followed by parties in student halls. And you know what I am left thinking? **Is this it?**

The truth is that there is no centre, no portal where all the decadence and glamour you craved opens up for you. There is just a lot of people standing about pretending they know where it is, pretending that they are part of its heart. At student art exhibitions, there's just a lot of people standing around, clutching paper cups to their chests, and hoping that their thin air of superiority will counter any accusations that they can't even offer any insight into their own art. There are other things, too. Geeky men in Clarks shoes, and the occasional almost-cute indie boy who glowers at you and then pretends they haven't seen you. No one tries to chat me up; I'm just a weird girl who probably has scary demon eyes.

In the party in the hall of residence kitchen there is no wild, bacchanalian orgy, or even a sense of seen-it-all wastedness that would suggest that the main event has passed. There is a semi-circle of bored people. One is fiddling with the CD player and one burning his fingers while he tries to make a roach. A total prick in a toga walks in and with public school confidence declares, "We're all going to play drinking games." You sit on a windowsill and let them get on with it, but it is all so inane that you can't even follow the action. You know what is so perverse, so fucked up? Not the fact that you can't even complain that people were trying to get off with you. But instead, the fact that at about 1am I look out of the small steamed window in the kitchen and realise I am actually missing home. **Tragic.**

In the first three days I can't even get up the nerve to phone Adam. It has been three days of sitting with my guitar, feeling unable to face my loneliness, let alone write about it. Why do I need someone else to make me feel I'm moving forward? It's ridiculous. Donna is still in Worthing and Melissa promises she will arrive any day now before the recording session we have booked. But I don't know how much practice I can do by myself. I have a dark feeling that the band won't get here in time for the session. And if the label has shelled out a load of money for nothing then we're going to get dropped. And the worst feeling? That there is nothing I can do about that. It's not as if I can sue my band mates if they ruin my career. It's not as if it'll affect their lives if they let me down. Anyone who actually hears my story will just shrug. It'll be the end of the only opportunity I've ever had, after months chasing these people. And having won them over, there'll be nothing I can do about it if they don't even bother to turn up.

In the last few days, I've been trailing around the warehouse bookshops and Iceland, buying bags of frozen stir-fry, waffles and frozen lasagne. A lot of times I can't actually face eating in the kitchen, so I torture my mouth with layers of hot and cold microwaved lasagne on my desk, while listening to John Peel. At one point, Adam's band come on and I feel like the universe is bullying me. I think of his fingers all over his guitar, all over other women. I wonder if I should tell Clare and Marie about my secret link to the pop underworld, but I can't face giving away this secret and seeing that no one cares. Deep down I am still smarting that no one has asked about my guitar, but in fairness, it has barely left its case. I am annoyed. I have tokens for the shabby amusement park ride comprised of support slots, backstage parties, and sex with men who are in magazines and I am not cashing it in. I am pointless.

I am in my bedroom when I make the call. My eyes trail over the string of fairy lights I have strewn over the sink in the

*corner, the dressing table with the ballerina music box, the
Blanche Dubois makeup puff, the silver vintage handheld
mirror and the eyeless dolls behind it all. They look at me
blankly, grieving for the sadness of their mother. That's what
they do-they watch me turn myself into a woman and they look
confused about what I am becoming. I sing the first line of
Hole's Doll Parts to myself. I try hard to look girlish, but I am
far more tired than I could ever let alone.*

*It is dark outside. I tell myself I am in control of my
emotions when I call Adam, even though I can't bear the
devastation I will feel if he doesn't answer. I tell myself he **will**
answer.*

*I now know that you should never chase someone when you
feel low. It's like they pick up on your vibes, and if the chase
doesn't work, you'll then sink lower than ever. So yeah, that is
exactly what happens and there is no one I can talk to about it.
His phone rings just once then says, 'Welcome to the Orange
answerphone.' The sinking feeling is horrid, and I know it'll
cling to me for days, like the smell of wood varnish.*

*It's a feeling enhanced by the mocking jubilation of the toga
wearers charging down the hall outside. None of them are
aching for someone to get in touch. None of them are checking
their phone every five minutes, completely unable to believe
how they haven't heard a single word from someone.*

*I cannot believe how exposed I have made myself just to feel
as if I exist. All I wanted was a shred of something to confirm
that my feelings were not madness, but that I actually had a
reason to take a huge leap. Now I wonder if it was all a
delusional figment of my imagination.*

*I can't think of anything to do other than sit on the bed and
cry. I am completely out of ideas.*

Tucking the diary deep into the rucksack, I thought about
Emma's experience with her band mates. I had always envied
her little gang but had no idea how fragile their union had
been. To me, they'd been a closed little group, bordered by
amps and a forcefield of private ambition. They had looked
unbreakable, and yet Emma had in fact thought of them as

ready to walk at a moment's notice. Without her talent, how would I ever convince people to join me? And yet, I had to now face that Emma had not been convinced of her talent, however clear it had seemed. She had acted as if she was convinced by it, while in fact being anything but.

Is that what I had to do, I thought? How else would I ever think myself worthy of people's attention?

Chapter Twelve

Melissa is there before you, all freckles and shining forehead, when you arrive at the studio. You could kiss her for her enthusiasm, especially when she says, as if it is obvious, "Donna is just parking round the back."

And she is, in the pub car park. Donna carries a fastidious and business-like air as, in a sleeveless shirt, she unpacks drums from her boot.

I briefly fret over where Simone is, but soon realise that I can play her bass parts if she deems this whole thing to be beneath her.

The studio has damp on the walls, and on a torn carpet milk crates prop up the amps. Stretched tights are used as pop shields over microphones. As we set down our tools, a portly man in a stained Grateful Dead t-shirt stands over us and stuffs his hands in his black jeans with an embarrassed smile. "We're all on time, then," he says, sarcastically.

I decide not to criticise Simone's absence, suspecting it'll be the start of a standard male divide-and-conquer tactic. And I will not allow a man that foothold on us. I lay my leopard print coat down like it is my bed which, in a way, it is.

I am sick to the back teeth of men believing that by withdrawing something they are in control of me. It makes me physically ill to think of Adam still having not replied to me in two days, given it was him who dropped all the hints about us. He was the one with the aching expression when I left, he found everything I said so incredibly funny that he didn't stop smiling the whole time we were together. And yet it's him who has deemed that in two whole fucking days I don't warrant a single word of reply.

As I slash some chords and try to tune my guitar, it sears into my memory. All those times he complained about how lonely he was. And then, when someone tries to throw in their lot with him, he just responds by pretending they don't exist. All that talk about how insincere people are, and how different he is, and how he feels things so acutely, and yet I give away a little of myself, and where is his sensitivity now? It's not remotely apparent in how he's treating me here. Even if he does reply it could well be in some dismissive remark to snidely let me know that I've got the wrong idea about us. A classic male strategy, flirt and then pretend you don't know where the assumptions have come from the minute you don't feel like playing any more.

So frankly I'll be fucked if sweaty Mike thinks he can get on top of us because fucking Simone missed the fucking bus.

He sits behind the screen which separates the performance room from the control booth. His expression teeters between an accepting smile and an acerbic put-down that you just know is coming.

As we tune up, I come to suspect that he is not completely thrilled to have been assigned to record the first single of a four-piece girl band that no one has heard of. I can see he cares little of our cult status but that commissions like this are his bread and butter. From my gut, I want to prove we are not some here-today-gone-tomorrow enterprise. I don't know how to do that though. I know nothing. After all, I can't even get a bloke to reply to me when I've moved cities to be with them. I try not to think what I'll say when my mum next asks how Adam is.

I can live with a lie, but I can't bear hearing yet again how I was naïve to express any faith in a man. I despise how Mum expects me to open up to her about the wreckage of my love life and yet in nagging me for news about it then wallows in my latest disappointments. Here's me trying to make a life for myself and all the universe repays me with is tardy band mates and men that won't reply.

*So I gulp, and try to push down into my stomach what all this says about my (lack of) talent and attractiveness. The fact of the matter is I can't **afford** a sense of pride. People in my* life are only in any way reliable when they are actually in the room with me. The minute they are not in the room with me, ideas about loyalty, professionalism, kinship, intimacy and friendship offer zero guarantee I will ever see them again. I am on the bottom rung of the ladder of influence. My dreams of creating a place for like-minded girls to find themselves have never seemed so distant. People are too unreliable. When it comes to Adam moving cities to be with them offers zero guarantees they will bother to reply to a message from you. Shared tears? Sex? Promises? Get it together, Emma. No one feels like they owe you a thing as a result of any of those. Good reviews, coverage, record deals, public admiration. None of it inspires them to reply to you and turn up when agreed. No one likes the person with ideas, and right now my precious ideas are just something to have sung back to me in the playground when it all collapses.

I think of the three weeks Melissa had my demo, when I told myself she hadn't got back to me over about joining the band because she was too busy, only for me to then pass a diner and see her eating ribs with a hen do, as if she had all the time in the world, as if it was all just a big buffet to her. I remember losing it, going in there to confront her and her turning to face me at the bar, me asking if she had listened to my demo yet and the way she measured and calculated my value with darting eyes, all in one second. Before she decided I had something to offer her, and she smiled. Then there was a meeting where four girls sat round a table and we all considered each other and sniffed each other and finally decided that we did have something to offer each other after all. Being dissected like that, it was horrible. It stung. All my girlfriends ever do is talk about how much pain they're in but they totally forget how much pain they are causing. To them that's just an annoying irrelevance.

It all stings. Every humiliation just illuminates, like a row of promenade lights, all the other rejections and betrayals that snake into the darkness of your past. You only think that record deals, gigs and minor fame create a net that will hold your life because you are on the outside of the net. It doesn't hold shit.

All you have is what people are doing in the room with you now. And knowing that hurts.

It hurts so much that in the past few days I have been unable to speak to anyone. It hurts so much that I have just walled myself off in my room and tried not to see anyone. And the moment I left the house and got bumped into in the street, all the hurt comes back. It hurts so much that at night the sense of betrayal is so huge it makes my heart pound. I have been making lists of people that have let me down and people who haven't. The first list is always longer.

I have started to adorn these lists with plans of what I will do to get my revenge on each of them. Next to most of their names is one word. SUCCESS. This single will be released by a cool label and get rave reviews. I will bury my hatred for Adam and claim him as my boyfriend. I will then be on the front of NME, arm in arm with him. And all the women that cozied up to me and then stabbed me in the back, and all the men who dumped me will see that I am a star and they can just choke on the ashes. The people who hurt me will all come crawling back and then I will tell them all-in pithy lines I have long rehearsed-what I really think of them. My pain will interest them then, because it will be all they can grip onto to try and get me back into their boring lives.

When did it all get so painful? When did my innocent ambitions about art and sharing turn so ugly?

A hot stream of sunlight through the window jolted me back to the present. So that was why she wanted success. To contribute to other people's lives. It wasn't *just* about ambition, after all. The line about Emma feeling so hurt she felt unable to speak to anyone was like something I'd write in my own notebook.

Perhaps the two of us weren't so different, after all, I thought. I decided to treat myself to a few more pages before the social horror show of the evening ahead, to try to find out what Emma did about those feelings.

Chapter Thirteen

When I returned to her, she was still seething.

Somewhere, behind all this anger and hurt, I know that I will start to see something approaching loyalty only if I push through all this self-pity and keep working hard. I know I have to conquer this dizzying sense of emptiness, and then I have to keep going. I know that after a few good reviews, and a few men flirting with me in front of Adam I'll start to see something from these people that is at least in the shape of loyalty. Even if it is not the real thing.

Talking of loyalty, when Simone finally arrives Donna's eyes work over her like she is planning a dissection and Simone has the good sense to allow herself to be pinned. I look at Simone, with that rakish glance girls throw when they consider another girl's imperfections. I am mildly perturbed to find none. Her skin is flawless, and her hair is rich and thick.

"Well cheers for coming, Simone," Donna says, her voice dripping in sarcasm, to make things clear.

*The thing is that Donnas know they need Simones and Simones know they need Donnas. If we were all as beautiful and flaky as Simone, the band wouldn't actually have an engine, but if we were all as no-nonsense as Donna, no one would fancy us. Girls like Simone need to learn to appreciate girls like Donna, as Donnas have got used to Simones decades ago. I think Donna knows I have a foot in both camps. I **think** I do have a foot in both camps. I'm Kristen Pfaff.*

I am so relieved there is one less missing person in my life that I offer her a consoling smile. Am I moving in the right direction? When Donna addresses a split drumstick with the words, "You useless bitch," we all know she is really talking about Simone.

I can see why boys fancy Simone, with all those long bones and willowy gestures, but they don't realise that getting in a relationship with someone like her would be like buying a book of really toxic poetry and being forced to recite it out loud every night. Simone has tried to get the band to play her songs, an idea that was soon shut down when we heard her fiddle heavy numbers which she sang in Old English. It was like something Geoffrey Chaucer scrubbed out with a quill when composing The Canterbury Tales. But it was only when she started singing the word thee that Donna finally said "enough".

But this remark reminds Mike he is dealing with a proper woman and makes him less likely to start sniping at us with his recent male accomplice (some tea boy with big spots on his neck). From this side of the glass I dare to feel like this is my gang. We are finding a way to talk to each other. We all know Donna rolls up her sleeves to show her biceps. We all know that Simone will burst into tears if you use the same criticism of her three times.

The fact is that my music is good enough to allow me to recruit three hot young women, with some talent and lots of style, and a small record deal. It has been good enough to secure a producer who once made an EP with a Japanese girl band I love. If we get it right, then what we make will be in shops. Although I have no idea whether it is dedication or mercenary ambition that has made the Cherub swarm around me all I know is that my shoulders start to lift during the few hours we pound through the first three tracks of the demo.

Donna is all flailing drum splashes, screams at her own mistakes, and shark-like grins of happiness as her cymbals fade. Simone churns out basslines in a sultry way, but I can see she is still embarrassed by her tardiness and will need a few takes to get going. Melissa is actually kind of brilliant. She has been working on her guitar lines and must have adjusted her sound over many weeks to come up with something so distinctive. It is a relief to see I am not the only one who silently plots alone in dark rooms. It makes me shiver with happiness to hear what she has prepared.

What was once a thin guitar solo has become a cacophony of swinging, sawing notes, that enunciate my melodies and make them so catchy. I have this sudden daydream. Us playing this song on David Letterman, Melissa offering angelic swoops of backing vocals behind my impassioned and uniquely memorable performance. I love the idea that I've helped these women finally express their gifts. If Mike does not compliment the songs, he grudgingly concedes they are ready to record because his questions from the control room opposite are perfunctory. "Can you hear all of the drums? Are you loud enough in the monitors?" At one point, as we record the first song, he refers to the bridge. The fact that he is conceding our songs have bridges, like real songs, makes me feel a long way from the teenager trying to play Bruise Violet on a guitar in my parents' front room.

Soon we start to layer the tracks. Donna gets down a drum part for the lead track that she is happy with, and her smiles lift everyone. Some people are ballast to the rest of the room, and people either have that charisma or they don't. Melissa, I realise, has practiced three or four different solos for each track. All are glorious, sexy and melodic. I worry about my vocals, the band on the other side of the glass listening in while sat on the milk crates. But having practiced them a lot on lonely walks, I am delighted to hear how I sound. I sound unique, gnarled, plaintive, but like no one else. "Not bad," Mike says, after a take, and I am so happy I would kiss him. Then I remember that all he has actually said was, "Not bad".

After all this, my emotional upswing makes me believe I am in the right state of mind to check my phone to see if Adam has replied. I pull my mobile from my guitar case.

Still Nothing.

*As if I need to lower my expectations about romance any lower. As if I **can** lower them any further.*

"Let them wait to hear from you," Donna says, passing behind me. With her, most of the conversation happens without words, with the real words bubbling away under the used ones. With her, it's all in the width of her posture, the pauses in her

breath, the nursing she does with her eyes.

She sits down behind me, and I realise I'm going to get the "talk". She looks back into the studio and lowers her head to me. I wonder if she's going to kiss me, or thump me, as if both are the obvious next steps in our relationship. "Another thing," she says. "Girls like Simone will come and go. You can't build a career on them. You need to have 'bottom'."

"What's 'bottom'?"

Donna smells of hair oil and mint. The other girls smell like talc and thundering, dreadful female pain.

"Bottom," she says, straightening her spine. "A big fat base of ideas and ambitions. And you need to work on all of them at once. And when one person lets you down you just move onto the next idea. We're not like Mike in there. People don't mistake a woman's surliness for skill." She inspects the tip of a drumstick. "We have to work four times as hard."

"Right," I say, impressed. It sounds exhausting, all that hustling, all that clarity.

"You're the only one of us that can have a public life."

"A public life?"

"You can be a star. You can headline Glastonbury. You can get people to write to NME complaining about your new haircut." She loses patience and waves her hands. "You do know what I mean, Emma?"

It is nourishing to feel mentored. I'm starving for it. And after this little morsel she leaves me alone with all my fear and doubt.

I think about how people don't just screw you, cry in your arms, cuddle up to you in the dark and then abandon you. They don't just take part in an exchange, which you both agree is incredible, and then not reply to you. They don't just nag you to move cities to be with them and then pretend the conversation never happened. You pull yourself out of all that hurt, do something truly productive and then return to your phone thinking you've done enough to warrant at least a reply.

And still nothing.

There are still a few hours of studio time left when the girls, satisfied they have recorded their little purls, start to go home.

My anger about Adam is twisting inside me. It's a dark banshee whose scream will be heard the moment I open my mouth. Mike is the only one left. He looks up at me from the desk and says something, with a tone I can't measure. "What now?"

Without thinking, I blurt out, "I'm going to record a few more songs." It's me who speaks, and not the banshee, but I know that the second I start playing she is going to get her turn.

He looks at the clock on the wall. He's thinking of warm pints in the pub and packets of Scampi Fries. But for all his dismissiveness of me, he simply can't dispute that I have a right to use every moment that the label has paid for. "Just you and a guitar?" he says, his voice wavering.

"Yes," I say, feeling my spine straighten. "If we set it up so I can record a few acoustically, I'll run through a few of them."

"A few?"

"Five."

He takes a deep breath, but I hold his gaze. He shrugs, and he starts unwinding the cord around a mike. He positions it so he can place over the hole in my guitar. I find a stool. This is happening. My banshee is being heard.

*I record Hairy Food, Girl Germs and a silly song called Medusa. I feel freer than I did with the band around me and the banshee cuts lose. Every drop of emotion in those recordings is about Adam. I scream, wail, and croon as the songs demand. They are a bit frightening, but they are definitely different. I have only ever sung them, my voice low, in halls of residence, so even I don't know what my voice will do at full stretch. My voice shocks, disappoints and impresses me. I don't have much range, but I have a lot of **emotional** range. Mike has no discernible reaction to the first song, but some of my lines in the second seem to make him smile. He tugs at his beard, thoughtful, without saying anything. The smiles have long gone by the time we start on the third. There is twenty minutes of studio time left and I am clinging to it like a shattered life raft with only a few planks left. "Right," he*

*says, standing up and smoothing his belly. "I need a drink.
Shall I leave the tape running?"*

"Yes."

*A week later the record label is surprised that instead of us
turning in enough for an EP, they are given nine tracks. Even
if five are without the band and they later required someone to
edit them from one long take I recorded while Mike sipped
John Smiths in a deserted pub garden. Shelli at the label calls
me says she found my solo tracks "dark, hysterical, brilliant".
Something blooms in my chest when I hear those words. I
wasn't convinced Mike was even going to send them on.*

*Adam replies two days later, when I have pretty much
healed up over the whole thing. It seems like that is the way
the world works. You never get what you want when you are
most excited and capable. What you want comes eventually,
dressed in its shabbiest state, when you don't even want it any
more. Or when without it things would collapse for others. At
first, the flashing of Adam's name in digital black on the
yellow screen creates a sense of contempt in me. Then the
phone shivers to life with a shudder that feels like destiny
calling. It's too hot and loud to refute. In a moment of panic,
I'm scared of missing this opening. I answer right away.*

*Adam sounds small. He doesn't ask how my recording
session went, even though I had mentioned it so many times. I
don't dare to snidely bring it up, and hint that some moral
support from a fellow musician, let alone a boyfriend,
would've done me the world of good. No, I just stave off the
white elephant in the room until, his voice shaking, he invites
me to see a band called Ashtray Cult. He promises that they
are "not bad".*

*As if not bad is the peak of anything we should ever hope
for.*

*But not bad is more than enough for me. I have fuck-all
options. I pretend to consult my diary, full of endless beauty
appointments and dates with other famous men before
discovering a window that exists at the exact time he's invited
me out. So no matter how much I resent him I jump at
whatever he offers. I can't even explain how much seeing him,*

and being in a venue, and getting the chance to be around real musicians will mean to me. I know that if I can somehow get beyond the sense of resentment, hate and hurt I might be able to twist this experience into the sense that I am finally where I want to be.

"How does that sound?" he asks.

"Not bad," I answer.

I stand in front of the mirror in the tattered bra and off-white knickers I was wearing and decide what to do with this girl so that she can give me what I want. I have a little bit of a tummy (from all the noodles) but then so did Marilyn. My feet are a tiny bit long and my nose is a tiny bit snubbed and freckly. I pull on a tight, sparkly black dress, foundation, eyeliner, glittery eyeshadow in the mirror over the sink. I hack at my hair until it curls how I want it to and then I put a silver clip in it. I paint my toenails red, and then push them into my Doc Marten boots. I put lipstick and lip-gloss on. I feel all last bus from Liverpool Street, cheap paperbacks on the Southbank, afternoon pints in Camden roof-gardens. I put on my leopard print fake fur coat and I am complete.

The self-centred, disingenuous, inexplicable bastard meets me at the Tube station by the venue. I round a corner and see him and, after a split second's insight into his own solitude in which I see endless self-hate in his eyes, his expression changes and he greets me with a loose hug. He then takes me in, and his smile suggests amused approval.

His body feels ridiculous in its thinness and his hair smells of cigarettes. But somewhere in the awkward geometry of his smile is the man I have come to this city for.

As we walk to the venue, he talks about the tour he has coming up, about the album his band is making in the studio. It somehow becomes a relief that he does not ask about me. Besides, how could I possibly share how torrid the last few days have been? How can I admit the huge role he's played in my private agony?

Looking at him as he talks, seeing his confidence oscillate as his stories falter between the compelling and the mundane, I realise he is nothing more than a shifty, uncertain, damaged *bloke in his late twenties. It is so pointless hating him; he is not able to act in a way that he can live with, let alone anyone else. I realise I should not have invested so much in him. I don't know how I created such castles in the sky from so little. Why did I hate someone so human? At least he is here now.*

The gig is held in the sticky backroom at the pub. As we go in, I see that the stage is made up of a series of stools and a table filled with instruments. Behind them, wooden chairs are stacked in preparation for the next event. A church group? With a tense air of silence, we lean against the empty bar at the back and I feel such a sense of relief to see the Gothic girls and the men with their dreads turn to look at us as we settle. One or two note Adam, and that I am his accomplice. I have gone from being nothing, and crawled, on my hands and knees, through cut glass, towards being something.

The music being performed is a strange stew of acoustic guitars over which a lyric about illicit sex is mewled by a goblin-like woman with a dark bob. But for all this shabbiness, I have to try as hard as I can to not beam with delight. If there is a scuffed centre to this world that I have been seeking, I might at least be on the outer rim of it now. My happiness is so great that I find myself, with Adam, smiling at certain lyrics. As if I am savouring and appraising them, as if the words people pour out into their songs in the back rooms of pubs actually mean something. Did I have to endure that recent agony to feel part of a scene? So I could become part of a group where people make things worthy of consideration? Have I now paid the entry toll? If so, I didn't know that was what I was doing! But in a way, it kind of feels worth it. Jesus, the price we pay to stave off loneliness, to feel part of something that doesn't make us ill.

A tall man next to the singer plays bass and, when the singer finally says, "Thank you, we've been Ashtray Cult," I realise the he wasn't a woman, but a man.

After the show the goblin greets Adam with a handshake. When he speaks, he has a strange Mid-Atlantic drawl, nasal and whiny. "Oh my god, I'm so stoked you came," he says, turning to me, "and who is this?"

"This is Emma, the singer from Cherub," Adam says.

I am smiling so hard at that introduction that my face has started to ache.

"Enchanted," the singer says. "Are you coming out to play tonight? Do you dabble?"

I don't know what this means. But I am Emma, singer from Cherub. I feel it in my stomach, my womb, and in the tips of my fingers.

I have finally made it to London.

So Emma didn't live in a magical world of constant coolness. She had to force it into being, with whatever scraps she had around her.

This thought sticks with me as I start to get ready for the night ahead.

Chapter Fourteen

I remember arriving at the campsite that evening, tired, carrying a rucksack full of meagre possessions and a strong sense of absurdity. After having spent so much time avoiding people, how could I now sleep with a bunch of them on a beach?

On a patch of sand, which sloped down the sea, a group of people my age were setting up tents for the night. Hot from the bus, I didn't allow myself to join them just yet. People are too painful to be around, I thought. There's nothing to gain from them; only things to lose.

People had noticed me and had been talking about me. I could tell by the way that everyone dropped what they were doing when they saw me, before gathering around. Ruth was different, though. She held onto the sticks in her arms and seemed to want to see me interact with other people before she said hello. Introductions were made. Although no one admitted that they knew who I was, the lingering glances betrayed that they did. It was a group of fifteen-year olds, their hair blonde from a relentless sun that had coaxed freckles onto their noses.

That evening everyone clustered around the campfire on the beach. Clumsy attempts to light portable barbeques led to charred sausages. Burgers were a safer bet. They spat and blistered and were prised between floury baps (any attempt to toast them just lead to more burning). At least we had something hot in our stomach. I sipped a bottle of warm beer, enjoying the sense of camaraderie. Some of the people were even younger than me and I felt an inexplicable guilt. Was I a joke for sharing beers with people in the year below? Ruth's presence, as she sat static opposite me, made me feel assured. I asked myself what I would do if she stood up and announced all this as childish, before going home. The options that presented themselves to me made me realise how unmoored I was. What was I really capable of, if left to my own devices?

I sipped the beer and had to acknowledge there was a void inside me. I couldn't even bring myself to smile at people and make conversation because I knew that any perceived rebuff was going to send me into a wild solitude, lasting weeks. I had to face up to the fact that I was teetering, and that Ruth was the only person who could pull me back from the brink.

The moisture that flicked through the evening was thrown up from the sea, the breeze whirling around us. The glow of the fire created an orange half dome that lit the young faces around it. Rising winds heightened the glow and then allowed it to fade. It was as if the wind was the host of the night.

We pushed marshmallows onto twigs. I smiled at Ruth and, when I fetched a beer for her, she said thank you, as though I'd saved her life. While a boy called Sam struggled through a Smashing Pumpkins cover on a stickered acoustic guitar I settled at her side. She put her head on my shoulder. "Where's River?" I asked, in a voice so soft I hoped it wouldn't discourage her from cuddling up to me. "Over there," she sighed, as if he was a mischievous labrador. He was doing backflips by the ocean for a crowd of admiring girls. Seeing his exuberance made me feel a little bolder.

"Come round here," I said, and I moved my legs around her back. "Oh, okay," she said, raising her head. I felt a pulse of erotic excitement as she lay between my legs, her head pressing against the inside of my shoulder. No one objected. No one pointed and laughed at the fact that I was cuddling up to someone. She didn't react with outraged disgust. The sea kept churning and the bonfire kept sparking, but I felt soothed. The fire lit a thin margin of fabric above Ruth's shirt, and lit the tiny hairs on her arms. When she held her bottle of beer out in front of her it looked as if the fire was dancing on top of the liquid inside.

Those few hours that Ruth lay on my shoulder flew past. I felt as if the summer I had longed for had finally arrived, a milky, warm, easy sensation, in which laughter and ocean were constant companions. All the things I had needed to say to someone now seemed less urgent. I savoured the smell of her hair, and the sound of her laughter when people near us exchanged jokes. I noticed how no one bothered me when I was cuddling up to a girl.

"You know, you can hang out with other people if you want," she said, at one point.

"I'm happy here," I said, and she accepted the answer enough to not raise the issue again. It amazed me to have something good happen without me feeling like I had to drag it out of the soil.

That night, Ruth retired early, sharing a tent on the beach with two young girls. She looked at me for a long time before retreating into her tent, and I waved my hand at her in a weird salute before I went into mine. In the morning I found the wet interior of River's tent and the way the morning sun pressed through it unnerving. But the blast of the sea, waiting to greet me as I unzipped the tent, cleansed any sense of dirtiness.

I stepped outside the tent and stripped down to my boxers. With my clothes a small pile on the sand, and with a borrowed hand towel at the ready, I stepped into the waves. They were wild and uneven. But the frothy water was cool, biting even, and once I took the plunge and threw myself into the water it rendered my flesh pale and thin. Seeing a large, transparent wave coming above me I decided to brave it and throw myself into the surf. I snatched at the sky and dived back down, where no one could reach me. Underwater, the sea was a sandy expanse, the surface a ridged white slope. When I broke to it the taste of salt on my lips and the cry of seagulls made it all feel embracing. I kicked around, trying to ease all the dirt from my body.

When River called me in I emerged, dripping and victorious. I felt like a hero of the beach. "We've got to carry this stuff to the car park and then walk home," he said.

"All the way round the harbour? That's miles," I said.

"Unless you want to run?" he asked.

I was comforted by the idea of a long walk with these people, who at that moment felt like my own tribe. This strange blend of man-children, with braids in their hair and bracelets on their arms. With t-shirts that said 'Animal', 'Stussy' and 'Fatface'. I hoped that if I stayed with them Ruth would join me on the walk. I had a feeling there was a conversation that needed to be had.

Chapter Fifteen

Once the kit was packed away, I joined the trail of bodies winding their way on the pavement around the harbour to the village. Where the view of a clay-lined bay, on which beached boats were stuck askew, was broken only by the whoosh of cars driving into the village.

The pavement was thin, and although on one side the empty harbour, with its dank scent of seaweed, had a strange charm, the passing traffic made the walk an unnerving experience. It exaggerated the sense that this could all end in a moment.

Ruth was a couple of feet behind me, chatting to a French student called Isobel, as I took in the dilapidated boathouses. They had mystical, New Age names. I saw an Osiris, a Meridian, and a Luna. Outside them plastic statues, gnomes or "No Vacancy" signs suggested chaotic lives within tiny chambers. We passed marina shops full of sleek speedboats on slats, impassive and powerful as Damien Hirst's sharks in Formaldehyde. Against these worn out shop facades the millionaire playpens looked pristine and preposterous. My thoughts were just beginning to tighten when Ruth joined me at my side.

"I was hoping you'd do that." The words were out of my mouth before I had even realised I was thinking them.

"Would you find it strange if I told you that I found you totally intimidating?" Ruth asked.

From the Brading Haven Sailing Club back to her house was a long walk, even on a balmy summer evening. The retreating tide made the clay and silt in the bay glisten. It was as if thin seams of diamonds were woven into the hollowed-out harbour. As we slipped into step with each other I realised the air had a mellow warmth to it, which felt magical. But as I had nothing to compare this feeling to, I was yet to know it was special.

I felt like a margin was being opened in the world, a realm of new possibility. As I worked out how to reply to Ruth, I felt as if the right choice of words, and the right resonance around them would allow immersion into that zone. It was strange; even though I knew I had slipped into a situation which I would come to see as timeless I would not have had the words to admit that to myself at the time. I did not even know that the exciting, pulsing feelings I was experiencing would fade as I got older.

"Why would you be intimidated by me?" I asked.

As we passed the boathouses, her smile seemed so sensual it was almost obscene. "Well, you're the brother of my heroine, for a start. I hope you don't find me saying that too disturbing."

I wasn't sure how to react.

She somehow sensed the openness of my reaction and was sharp enough to pick up on the sense of connection between us.

"You idolised her because of her music?"

"Yes. And by what she represented, what she could have represented."

Frankly I felt relieved to be around someone that could articulate themselves. Was I really going to tell her about the diary? Ruth was nodding, which encouraged me. But I said to myself, not yet.

"I don't know what you'd call it," I continued. "Guts, charisma, self-awareness. But Emma made things happen, and there are so few of those people in the world."

She was still nodding.

I concentrated on my feet. "And when they go, it leaves a hole."

Ruth waved her hands as if wanting to cradle my skull. "Exactly," she said, "I'm so glad you know what I mean. Even though at the time I was a bit scared of her I now just kind of want to *be* her."

"Sure."

She blanched. "I mean, I want to live in London, be in a band, have that lifestyle."

I nodded. Did I share what I had read in the diary? Life was pulsating through me. I decided to try.

"I've been reading the diary she left behind," I said.

Nothing happened. There was no thunderclap, no elemental moment of judgement. The water in the harbour didn't rise up to stop me speaking.

"And what has it revealed?" she asked. She was dancing a step ahead of me now.

"How much she struggled. How much everything people admired about her had been fought for tooth and nail. How nothing came easy to her, despite how it looked from the outside."

"Wow. You know, I just want to live in that feeling of possibility she made. And I... associate you with that feeling. Like you and her are the same." She bit her lip. I got the sense that she was taking risks with what she was admitting now, too. It was an exhilarating feeling.

"Well, I used to know nothing about what she was really getting up to. But this diary. It's telling me all of it." I turned to face her. "I'm having to read it quite slowly. Because it's blowing my mind. It's all pretty painful. But she's also kind of teaching me a lot through it." I looked to the crawling traffic. "It's making me feel like I can do things."

"People see you as someone who does things already, Jeff. You know that, yeah?"

"I guess."

She was gesturing with her hands now, in a way I hadn't seen before. "That makes you fascinating to people. Don't you see that? They're scared of you, and morbidly curious too," Ruth said, our feet perfectly in step now.

"I suppose so," I said. "I need to shake off this idea that I'm just the disappointing brother. Maybe I'm just trying to live in the space she left."

"Is it weird that I'm doing that, and I barely even met her?"

I laughed. "I don't know. It takes a bit more work on your part though, as she got to release so little as an artist. Well, so little of what she had done." I paused and tried to work out how to shape the question I really wanted to ask. "What *do* you want to do, then?"

"So many things." I had never seen Ruth come alive like this and sensed that all that reading on the lawn was in preparation for moments like this. "I want to be the young girl in big, dirty London. Sleepless nights, gigs in basements, interviews in pubs." She caught my expression. "You're thinking that I don't exactly come across as someone who's hungry for life, aren't you?"

I shook my head. "I know you might *think* you come across as bookish, all Jane Austen novels and that, but I know there's so much more to it than that."

The smile on Ruth's face was sudden and dramatic. The image of the girl reading Sense and Sensibility on a sunlit lawn was fading into memory. In my mind she now had a fake fur stole draped over her shoulders, tacky red sunglasses and a Popsicle. What had happened? Had she become intoxicated by music at some point?

"So unlike River *you* actually acknowledge that I have a good taste in music?" she asked.

I thought of how the other morning I had heard the bluesy riffs of Ocean Colour Scene oozing from her bedroom. I'd gone into the garden and, under a web of shadow cast by the leaves, had put in my earphones and slipped into the psychedelic, trippy world of a Chemical Brothers track I liked. My mind had felt as if it was unhinging, uncurling.

"Who am I to judge?"

"I don't know." She tucked a lock of hair behind her ear. "The thing is, I see your family as kind of tastemakers."

"People think Emma had it all worked out," I said, tasting the smog from the road. "But what looked like good taste was just good instincts."

Ruth screwed up her mouth.

"It's funny," I said. "If you look you look at a record of hers, it seems like it's just a product of how she lived. But that's not it. All that stuff is at the outer limits of who she wanted to be."

"Then it's a mistake to think she lived in the world, and to envy her for it?"

"Totally. She was smart enough to know she needed to push any ideas she had to the very limit if she was going to make a mark on the world. She was working out who she was when she died. So now people look at her work and think she's in it. She's not. It's just that her *working out* is there."

"It didn't feel like working out. Remember when Emma's band came to the school?"

"Of course."

"She was mesmerising. I remember everything about it; I modelled myself on her that night."

When, I thought.

"I even bought the leopard print clip she had in her hair!" she continued. "Do you remember how when she came on she threw glitter over the front few rows? She said they needed a touch of glamour!"

"No," I said. "I don't remember that."

She looked at me askance, sunlight blasting through her hanging hair. "This is incredible, because you know the source of all this stuff that's shaped me." She shook her head. "It's like I'm getting this insight from the beyond."

"Well in that case you might like this. Did you know I'd written some of the words to the first song she did that night?"

"Ruined Beauty Pageant?"

I nodded. How did she know the name of it? I had visions of Ruth being one of the girls that stole my sister's set lists off the stage. In fact, in my mind it was somehow *her* who had stolen the set list at Camden.

"I didn't know you were a poet."

"Emma used to look in my journals for ideas." I felt a need to calm the twitching passion on her face, having worked so hard to rouse it. It was strange, for once *the truth* was having the effect I wanted it to have. I wasn't having to pretend to be someone else. "She stole a whole load of lines off me for her first London gig."

"You must have been so close. I'd love to go to London one time. To go to those venues."

The remark provoked an intriguing thought. On some plane of existence, did Emma still exist?

Ruth looked composed but I could see from the flicker of her eyes that her mind was racing. This was one of those conversations we'd both be replaying in future, no matter what happened.

"Maybe I'm trying to find Emma in all this stuff, just like you," I said. "The feelings I get off it are so strong. Sometimes I don't know where the memories end and the present begins."

"I know what you mean. Sometimes the past feels just so alive."

I smiled. Was I really going to tell her? Was I really going to tell her the extent to which I'd tried to bring Emma back to life in my mind?

"You could actually live that life if you wanted," I ventured.

Her widened eyes suggested I was pushing it. "As the front woman of a rock band?" she asked, incredulous.

"Or, you could live your own version of that life," I said.

"I know what you're thinking," she said. "You can't see me thrashing about in a basement in fishnet tights."

"I can see you in fishnet tights whenever I want to," I said.

"Can you?" she asked, with a smile.

"Yeah, in my mind."

To my surprise, she smiled back. I was relieved. I'd revealed that I did have urges, urges that I'd long tried to keep to myself, and that confession had been met with warmth. "Whatever floats your boat, Jeff," she said.

Chapter Sixteen

We both stopped as we reached the stone steps that wound up to the village. The very steps River had leapt up were the same ones Ruth stood at the bottom of. I suspected both of us were keen to somehow preserve the moment. I remember her standing, curling a lock of hair over her ear again. I had the strong feeling I was expected to seize the moment. I had no confidence in what women wanted me to say, but I was still feeling energised by the whole "fishnet tights" breakthrough. I opened my mouth but realised there was no way to form the bustling, burning thoughts in my mind into words. She was looking over my shoulder at the sea with this strange expression, her eyes narrowing. I could feel the moment running out.

"What are you thinking?" I asked.

"Well, I'm thinking we should take Brown Owl out for a bit," she said. She nodded to it, lying belly up on the sea wall to her right. Its hull was sparkling in the afternoon sun. It looked like a fish that had been pulled out of the ocean and flipped onto its back. River hadn't even bothered to cover it.

"He won't mind," Ruth said.

I knew it was a lie and she knew I knew it was a lie. As if inspired by the idea she rolled up her sleeves. The faint blush on her face told me that this moment of inspiration would fizzle out with a single hitch. I dragged the little thing down the slippery, dull gold sand. The water looked choppy, tips of the waves frothing white. Ruth threw her shoes into the boat and concerned herself with rolling up her jeans, yelping as the sea caught her legs.

"We're going for a row. We're bound to get a little wet," I said.

"True," she answered.

I tried hard to hide how much effort it was to row the boat out past the crescent of rocks and into the calmer waters. At the other end of the boat, Ruth pulled strands of brown hair from the corner of her mouth and laughed at me. We were getting nowhere, and it took me a while to find a rhythm. She looked at me in a way that suggested she knew I needed help but that she'd decided it best to let me work it out.

The oars chopped in the water and we started to drift towards the sun. It was a curiously satisfying feeling, overcoming a problem on my own but knowing someone was there to help me if I failed. As I pulled the boat into the smooth waters over a sandbank, I made the most of the breakthrough, pulling the oars inside and falling dramatically onto my back. The boat began to drift.

"Wow," she said, trailing her fingers in the water. At my end of the boat I did the same and watched the oil from my skin form little slipstreams. The water was startlingly clear. I saw tiny shoals of silver fish darting in secret arrows. Ruth's attention was caught by something in the water, and when I asked her what it is she pulled out a long column of seaweed. The seaweed was wrapped, like a claw, over a beautiful blue pebble. A spiral of water caught me as she pulled it into the boat.

"What's that?" I asked.

"It's called a shooting star. Watch this," she said.

With a look of intense concentration, she stood up and whirled it around her head like a lasso. When she let it go my mind caught a camera shot of this falling stone, trailing water like stardust. It made a lovely plop sound as it fell into the water. Buoyed by her triumph, Ruth raised her hands in glee. But a wave caught us, and she toppled over. I darted over to catch her and she laughed, her mouth spreading into a warm smile as she fell in my arms. I caught the scent of coco butter on her skin, the fragrance of the sea in her hair. Her eyes locked onto mine. "Well," she said, widening them. "You just saved me from drowning."

I smiled. She looked at my mouth and I wondered if this

was really going to happen. But she seemed so warm, so inviting, that it felt like the most natural thing in the world to fall into the moment and kiss her. The wind wrapped her hair around my head as we kissed again. I felt ecstatic, as though I'd had this enormous breakthrough. Gulls cried overhead, as if agreeing. The next wave pushed me down and I found myself lying in her arms. As the sea rocked us, we began to relax and she ran her fingers through my hair. I looked up at the blistering sun and wondered if I'd ever felt so safe. Ruth hummed to herself, as if careful not to disturb me or the water. I imagined Brown Owl bobbing like a little cork on this huge ocean.

"You okay?" she whispered, smoothing my hair. I loved the sensation of being looked after. Something seemed to be opening in my chest. It was as if old, cracked, dried layers were being broken open.

"Even though I know this thing could tip over at any moment, I feel weirdly safe," I said.

"Aw," she whispered. She kissed me on the top of my head. "You are safe, Jeff," she said.

I remember closing my eyes. I knew that at some point I would have to find the strength to row us back. I knew at some point this experience would end and I'd be back to silence, and the diary, and all those burning questions that I couldn't answer. I tried to forget about it all, and let the sea take us where it wanted us to go.

I was awoken from my slumber by Ruth extracting herself from me and splashing the oars back into the sea. "The tide's shifting," she said. She focused on placing the oars deep into the water. "Besides how hard can it be?" she asked. "River can do it."

The mention of her brother froze me for a moment. What would he make of all his? I looked down into the water as she rowed us back. We pulled the boat back onto the wall and she kissed her fingers and patted its hull as we left it there.

We walked up the street I used to live on. I had never felt more protected; like I was embedded amongst a conspiracy of angels. I looked into the houses I'd walked past as a little boy.

It was all still there, I thought, it was just that I had left it for a while. It was a state of mind, I decided, and I could return to it at any time.

I thought of all the beautiful lawns, of all the trees with the owls nestling in them. I had cherished the sound of those owls during sleepy mornings. I thought about everything I had loved about this street as a boy. Sunlight poured through the trees and lit Ruth's face and she squinted at me and smiled.

I remember a little sequence that floated outside of time, as Ruth and I walked up that road. I didn't yet know that I would soon be living on that beach in a tent. If I had known how special those few minutes were, I'd have walked more slowly, and preserved them.

But as Ruth and I walked up the lane, shaded with a heavy canopy of green leaves, there was a sense of finality about it all. She and I barely spoke. As we walked into her driveway River ran to join us. Our exchanged glance gave me the distinct sense he was interrupting something important.

Even he saw it.

"Have you two been sharing your tragic life stories?" he asked.

"No," Ruth said, flashing red. "In fact, Jeff was telling me how he pictures me thrashing around in fishnet tights, actually."

River pulled off his shoes and started to tie the laces together. "How odd," he said, distracted.

"Odd that your friend thinks of your sister in that way, or odd that anyone finds me erotic?" she asked.

River put his arm around my shoulders. "Odd that you find my sister erotic," he said.

Ruth looked very vulnerable. I looked into River's eyes. "I'm afraid I do," I said.

Ruth went red.

"Freak," River said, sprinting away.

Ruth and I didn't speak, and when we walked into the house she said, "See you, Jeff," and retired to her world of impenetrable femininity. I went back to what I did not yet know was my final night in the annexe.

I was alone at last, but for once I felt strong with it. I was lifted by whatever had sparked between Ruth and me. It made me feel like a man made of flesh and blood for once, rather than a ghost. As I picked up her diary I didn't fear an outpouring of grief. I was strangely calm as I flicked through those pages.

Trying to work out what *I* should dedicate my life to made me think more deeply about the choices Emma had made. No one had encouraged her to form bands, so where had the determination come from? Was I lacking something necessary in not having that ambition?

When I realised the next entry was about the difference in how Adam and her were treated, I started to suspect that her ambition might've triggered her. She opened the entry with a question.

Is this what it feels like to have made it?

When Adam and I arrive at his recording studio (him in a ridiculously low-cut black V-neck, me dressed sumptuously in a matching black dress and shades) I realise the place is designed to make you feel like you have made it. Such places have to be luxurious enough to pull artists out of their own filth so that they can get something done. Something creative, which the suits are incapable of making.

The receptionist knows his name. Her smile remains fixed as she works out what studio he is in. As a girlfriend, I am persona non grata, but persona, nonetheless. The receptionist sways her hips as she takes us through to the control room. She does it in a way that makes even me look at her arse.

*So this is what recording studios are **supposed** to be like. The seating area behind the screen looks designed to house people with as much comfort as possible. To draw out of them as many songs as they have, for the world to savour.*

Ours looked designed to fit in as many milk crates as possible. It seemed a miracle that the place could be used to record music other people could actually hear.

You could be forgiven for thinking that the studio Adam's band is recording in is a spa, which just happens to have an air-conditioned, low-beamed recording studio as one of its features. It's evident that the rest of the band have been here a while. There are takeaway boxes, guitars thrown onto their backs, and the air-con battles to overcome stale breath. The bassist and singer greet Adam's arrival by clamouring round him for a range of telling hugs.

Leather creaks and ash is dropped. The bassist, Martin, hugs Adam like he is his little sister. "At least the photos will look good now," he says. He is all endless legs in white jeans and shark-like grins. The singer, James, tackles Adam like a terrier. The drummer, Mike, holds a stick aloft in greeting from the other side of the glass. "Alright, Emma love," says James, his words like the gasp of air before a huge cough. When he next opens his mouth it'll be to scream into a microphone on the other side of the glass. Neck veins popping, hands clenched. For now, he is circling his agony. Once he crosses the glass, he will place himself at the centre of it. Then it'll be like a volcano is flowing through him.

Adam settles in with a can of Red Stripe. The producer, indistinguishable from ours except for the better class of beard, looks warily at me. His expression wonders if I could possibly be more surplus to requirements.

I am here to learn. I already know that this is a band sliding into oblivion. I want to learn how that happens, to ensure my band instead rises like a phoenix.

It is only when an NME photographer arrives that I am allowed to come alive. Before then, I feel like any animation on my part will be treated by everyone with dread. It makes me wonder what kind of women Adam must have brought with him in the past. I picture lots of floppy hats, lots of silent glowering. Disruptive sulks. For male rock stars, women are part of the fun, and part of the difficulty.

The photographer is, of course, sultry, dark haired. Probably Belgian, but foreign enough to have an exotic air that I lack. It's pretty apparent what little perks come with being a male rock star, when beautiful arty girls keep snapping you from all angles in pursuit of their earnest craft, until you come (to believe) you are inherently fascinating. I just know

94

that if I wasn't here Adam would play up to her attention and God knows what would happen.

They all play up to her, with various cocks doubtless twitching in various jeans. As soon as her photographer's lens cap is off, Martin has his feet on my lap. Adam starts smiling, raising cans in her direction. The natural geometry of their body language, James' dominant stance, Mike's deathly focus, is exaggerated for the camera. Her pictures will form part of a narrative which declares that everyone involved had to overcome serious challenges to create the great record.

This is the lightest mood I have seen Adam in. He palms through lyric books in which words have been written so hard that the pages are like dry leaves. When the mix is played over the monitors the photographer starts snapping. But the truth is that the reaction is a negotiation that I can see happening on each of their faces.

James looks incandescent, and variously takes his frustrations out on the string around the beer crate, his guitar lead, and the sheaves of paper Adam has scattered on the floor. Martin acts as if this is all some ludicrous joke (which in a way it is). The drummer keeps banging throughout the playback, his muffled purgatory personifying something we are all trying to ignore.

The tension rises as the photographer keeps snapping, and the click of her Nikon starts to feel taunting. Interminable frustration is about to teeter into full-blown crisis. I realise that this is the feeling I associate with life. It's unnerving, unreasonable, endless. No one has the weapons to deal with the monster looming on the horizon. No one knows what form it will take, and no one admits it is there, but we all know it's coming. If only you could get everyone to join forces, they might be strong enough to handle it, but since when are people capable of joining forces? When the monster comes it will destroy us, and the rest of our lives will then be spent lamenting how it happened. The odds are stacked against us, as Adam always says.

The track sounds like cartoon punk rock. Thin, smothered in digital hiss, hollow. When you can make out Adam's anti-

capitalist lyrics, they just sound pompous against such a backdrop. It is the sound of compromise, but he is smiling. I wonder if his mind is really as sharp as I had assumed it was if he is happy with this track. Then I realise that something darker is going on.

It is only after an hour of sweaty indecision that Adam and I leave the room. We are in the spa with the hot wooden floor when he tells me what he is really thinking.

We've packed swimsuits. It feels like the wrong time for a dip in the pool. Me skinny and girlish, him pale, scarred and tattooed. The aqueous blue a shimmering echo on the whitewashed walls. I ask what he really thought of the track.

He dives, and then comes up for air. His black hair is plastered to his face. The water shows up shaving wounds, acne scars.

"The band didn't seem very happy," I say, coaxing.

The ridge above his lip filters water. "That's because it's cock rock bollocks. But at least they're using my words, not Martin's," he says.

"So what's the song about?"

He flips onto his back and starts swimming away from me.

"This woman called Kitty Genovese. She was repeatedly assaulted in front of a tower block in New York, and despite hundreds of people knowing what was going on none of them called the police."

"Well, as long as you're happy," I say, doing a backstroke.

He stands up straight. "Of course I'm not," he says. "The whole thing's going to shit. But with a label this big at least I'll have got a single that's about something into the top forty before we get dropped."

"And you're okay with getting dropped?"

He smiles. "It's not as if I have a choice. There are four people in the band, and they all have equally bad ideas."

"But you got this far."

He looks up at the ceiling as if he's seen a comet. "What a miracle," he says. "The thing is, people our age think you have to be really careful about what you say and do. They think at any moment with one wrong move you'll stop being cool and then that'll be the end of the world. But no one knows why they're cool so they don't know how they might lose it. The truth is that you could set yourself on fire and people will still forget you in a few weeks. So it's just not worth caring about."

Something about this obtuseness, this cynicism, unhinges me. "I thought you had a long-term plan. I thought you were... an artist," I say.

He swims away from me.

"What's there to be artistic about? These things have a shelf-life of two years max." He falls onto his back. "And rock stars only have until they're twenty-seven. By then they're fat or dead. Basically," he says, blowing at the ceiling, "my career plan is to develop a serious eating disorder."

I feel sick. There's me, using every scrap of studio time to get down every idea I've had, thinking it somehow matters when I have no audience. And there's him, with a salivating audience waiting all over the world and it's all nothing to him. It's just a petty little game of one-upmanship where his only motivation is to ensure he's not cheated of any opportunity. He isn't crafting anything. He has no belief in the redemptive power of art. It's all just another crock, as far as he's concerned. On a deep, fundamental level, he gave up long ago. This isn't the start for Adam. It's all part of the endgame.

At that moment I no longer envy him. At least I believe in **something**. It may well be out of reach, it may well be unrealistic, but it is something. I believe in the idea that you can find yourself through art. That you can make enough money to live off it.

He starts swimming even further away. "Look around you, Em. At all this. What on earth have any of us white kids done to deserve this luxury? It's just a sop to hide the fact that our youth is being exploited. The whole thing is pathetic."

If he wants to know about pathetic, perhaps he should've sat in on the fanzine interview I did after leaving his studio. This scintillating portrait of my artistic process took place in an Italian Café near Covent Garden. I waited half an hour, on a cramped table in the corner by the window, for my

97

interviewer. Looking out at people with real jobs, real lives. My elbows sticking to the table whenever I shifted in my seat.

Unlike Adam, I did not have snake-hipped temptresses bringing me beverages. I bought my own rank coffee and sipped it as slowly as possible, knowing I couldn't afford another one. When my interviewer finally arrived, he was unapologetic. College essays spilled from his rucksack and sweat bloomed in the armpits of his lumberjack shirt as he sat down. He looked too frail and pale to have cut down a tree in his life but was clearly going to have a go at felling me anyway.

One of the first thing he says, as he opens his notebook is, "I didn't get the chance to listen to your single. But I have a good idea what it sounds like, so don't worry."

"How do you know what it sounds like?"

He winces. "Well it's a Riot grrrl record isn't it? They all sound the same."

I sit back. "No, they don't. Riot grrrl was a movement in the US and although my music has a similar message..." I ran out of patience. "So how are you going to interview me if you haven't heard my music?"

His pen stabs at the notebook with a frustration he actually seems to think is sincere.

"Because this is a chance to tell the world what it is you want to do with your music."

"Sure," I say, folding my arms. "Our music is intended to show the world that young women are not just followers, part of a scene, inferior to their male counterparts. We have a lot to say and we believe our music is the most powerful way to say it."

His raises his eyebrows and says, "Fair enough. And do you all play your own instruments?"

"Yes. Do you write your own articles?"

"What do you mean?"

The remark has half caught him. I need a more direct hit.

"Well I just wonder if you'd have asked a male musician that question?"

Adam, I think. Would you have asked Adam that question?

Adam, who spent far less time learning to play guitar than I did.

"You're the girlfriend of Adam from Rosary, aren't you?" he asks, with a smile. "Has that helped your career?"

I close my eyes.

That night I find myself waist deep in the grubby rock and roll fantasy. We are in the same hotel where Prince stays when he is London. After the gig and the disco afterwards, in the basement of some hotel on the edge of town, my mood is as liminal as the location. We, the group and the members of its orbit (carefully policed by degrees of disdain from the group's rhythm section), are in such a shared state of narcissism that we don't even react when the DJ puts on the band's latest single. The band's smiles remain magazine fixed.

I realise, lingering on the edge of the dance floor, that the potency of my femininity has been rendered useless by the groups androgyny. My leopard print, my cosmetics, my hairspray-in this setting they are all a bad imitation of the groups aesthetic. Being feminine here is pathetically derivative, when it is their appropriation of the feminine (itself a snide appropriation of something they know to be divine) which is what is coveted here. I am just a semi-comatose disciple.

The record label's black cab takes us back to the glistening bronze, gold-lined mezzanine of the hotel room. In the lift, Adam takes pictures of us in shades as it ascends. My ripped fishnet tights wrap round his white fur coat, he glugs from a vodka bottle, winks at the camera from behind designer sunglasses. The pictures now linger on the floor next to my faded lingerie as I lie on the bed and write.

In the hotel room he pushed me onto the Egyptian cotton sheets, poured vodka onto my chest, tore off my bra and suckled on my erect nipples, licked the clear rivulets from my neck. He left a vicious hickie on me. He tried to take off his trousers, and I went down on him as he swayed on his knees. He is now in the hotel bathroom trying to vomit up the hamburger he ordered from a drive thru on the way home. We have been upgraded to the Presidential Suite, a Ballardian

99

nightmare of fake metal finishing and low circular couches that has housed more groupies than business meetings judging from the vague smell of semen and deodorant. From the bathroom I hear him swig vodka and then wretch into the sink. My body is covered in remnants of his body, but I remind myself that offers no guarantee of anything. By agreeing to be cast into this role I have agreed to be abused. I am mere cannon fodder in the ongoing war that rock 'n roll wages on meagre reality.

I have just done some of the poppers on the side of the bed and washed the effect with swigs of Red Stripe. He is singing the song of his that was played at the disco. I have just stumbled towards the circular sofas and looked out at the neon night. Bleak roundabouts, traffic lights through darkness and the fog of rain. The morning is a distant betrayal that's yet to happen. I have betrayed myself. I am an imitation angel, the disciple of nasty demigods, the temporary mistress of a spoilt prince next in line for the kingdom. I am photocopy of a woman, a groupie in an aborted narrative that I can never now escape.

I am about to lie down on the couch and hope no one touches me until morning.

Chapter Seventeen

The sunlight was making me see spots. I lay back on the double mattress, the thin sheets sprawled over me. I closed the book. Emma's last entry suggested that her relationship with Adam was taking a darker turn, and I wasn't able to take it just yet.

I lay back on the bed and tried to piece together the timeline. That entry must've been written a few days before Emma brought Adam to stay with the family when we rented a holiday home on the Isle of Wight. The first words on the next page confirmed I was right.

Dad picks us up from the Esplanade.

I could only remember fragments of that strange weekend. I remember the fear that Adam would be cruel and make Emma ignore me. I remember, as well, the fear that he would say something so provocative over dinner and then Mum would confront him. I'd had an ongoing concern that all Mum's anxiety around Emma would come out and result in flying plates.

Perhaps that's what should have happened. But what happened was very different.

Saskia and Charlotte visit. There's this awkward ten minutes where they don't seem to want to come further than the hallway, as Adam hangs on the stairs and they both play with Mum's new Scottie dog. I can't help noticing that neither of them has ever worn as much makeup, and Charlotte is wearing a PJ Harvey t shirt, curious given she never mentioned her before, and that in Adam's NME interview last week, he happened to praise her. I wonder if it has anything at all to do with the new fanzine Charlotte started days before my famous boyfriend would come to stay, one rather appropriately called 'Fear and Desire'.

Saskia is dressed like a full-time sculptress. A mound of dark curly hair piled on top of her head, tied up with a scarf. It almost makes me want to sleep with her, so god knows what it does to Adam.

Jeff, River and his sister Ruth splash in the pool. I can see them watching us through the poolroom windows as my gang make our way to the bottom of the garden. We sit on the wall behind the trees, overlooking the sea. It is so clearly our weed smoking spot. Parents who care would do something about it. Saskia says, antagonising me, "Shouldn't you clear some of these stubs away? Your Mum could find them."

At first I'm concerned with how dull Adam will find it to hang out with my high school friends. As he draws on a spliff, I try to work out what he thinks of the indoor pool, the not-yet-divorced parents, the garden with a view of the sea. Charlotte and Saskia chat much more than they ever had before. They've suddenly become very passionate about their art portfolios. Having skilfully mentioned her fanzine, Charlotte makes the most of the single question Adam asked about it to see if he'll be consent to being featured in it. With plenty of opportunities now for them to have conspiratorial conversations that don't include me I need to keep Adam close. I snuggle my head against his shoulder and whisper, "Are you sure you're alright?"

"Yeah," he says. "When I was a kid, we just drank cider in the park. This place is amazing."

I look up and go, "What, here?"

He looks incredulous. "Are you joking?" he asks. "You're so lucky. When I was a kid, I didn't have a beach to smoke on. Why would you ever want to leave this island? It's paradise."

Saskia and Charlotte are so shocked by this that their mouths hang open. The idea we are already in paradise is such a huge misunderstanding of what drives the three of us that it's kind of brilliant. And he's kind of right.

I have to admit a few things. The sea, pale and blue and flat, does look kind of magical. In the end we invite Jeff and River, who are playing football nearby, to join us. Ruth watches the whole thing from the deep end of the pool where she treads water.

"Can I have a puff?" Jeff asks.

"Aw," Charlotte says. "Your first joint?"

"No," he says, too casual.

"Are you sure we're not corrupting him?" Saskia asks.

I have this little flash of insight. I know Charlotte as the girl with the witch hazel stick in her handbag, who spends most of her time worrying about getting her hair pulled out again by the girls in the year above again. I think of her as the woman that refused to come out of her room when her first boyfriend dumped her, and for the way she only ever addresses her mother by screaming. But it scares me that one cool t-shirt, one leather jacket, and a non-existent fanzine later, she becomes this sexy, arty girl on the precipice of being discovered by the world. It is surely only a matter of time before Adam starts using this opportunity.

Being minded this way herself, Charlotte ruffles Jeff's hair. "Have you got a girlfriend yet?" she asks.

"No," he says, again.

Laughing, and looking at Charlotte, Saskia says, "Do you want one?"

Everyone laughs but Adam.

I know it's cruel, but where's the harm in it?

Ruth is standing at the window of the poolroom, watching us with a towel around her shoulders. She probably despairs at what girls like me represent.

"We should get ready for tonight," I say. "Before Mum brings the roof down."

'Tonight' involves an ill-advised acoustic slot I'm supposed to be doing at the inn on the edge of the harbour. One night after a few drinks there I'd been shooting my mouth off about my band-and-part flirting and part challenging-the owner had asked how I'd managed to make it without playing in his pub. Some beardy local chipped in, mentioning how he'd been paid

fifty quid to strum a few songs for the patrons there once, and I soon found myself talking the owner into a gig I didn't really want to do.

Even as I change into an appropriately demure dress for the occasion, I am torn between embarrassment at the thought of Adam watching me try to serenade a few villagers, and the awareness that I do seriously need the money. Charlotte has vaguely agreed to join me on stage, but I wasn't sure if she was serious. I am about to find out.

As I walk with Charlotte and Saskia and Adam down the hill to the inn, with Charlotte's semi-acoustic on my back, I try to work out which songs I know all the way through. I bitterly regret the days I have spent submerged in vague angst when I should've been practicing chord sequences. As we walk, sunlight filters through the trees on the side of the road. My accomplices are illuminated and darkened with each passing step. There are few things as beautiful as sunlight flitting between railings and onto you.

It occurs to me how irredeemably cool and beautiful my friends look. Their teeth are so white, despite all those cigarettes. Their lithe thighs are revealed by their summer dresses as they walk, their skin part tanned, part pale. They are the stuff of thousands of fantasies and they don't even know it. The light fuzz of hair on their arms is lit by the sun, making it look like they have auras. Their hair is so thick, and their smiles are so pure, plus Charlotte has these mannerisms that betray expensive schooling, like how posh boys, in a moment of inaction, kneel forward to do a fake cricket block, she tends to arch her hands above her head like a ballerina.

The girls don't realise how innocent they are, how no one is fooled by the smoking and the drinking. We are still all cherubs. It seems wrong that I'm not taking a picture of this moment, and I get the fleeting feeling that this group will not last very long. We are bound together by age and circumstance, but I suspect it will take little for us to go from holding and hugging one another to blanking each other in the very bar we're about to go to. I realise that a photo to capture this fragile union would be a precious memento. But I have no camera.

The local lads on their BMXs stare at us while we wait outside the venue. One of them places two fingers over his mouth and pushes his tongue through them at me as I pass. As we enter, we cluster together like a gang into the hushed silence. But I am the only one that moves to the raised dais behind the door. I try to act as if I know what I'm doing amongst the wires and stools. Looking around, I see there are more people in than I had expected, friends of my parents, people from school. Surely they can't be here to see me.

I plug my guitar into where I think it belongs, knocking over the mic stand that's been set up in the process. I pull it upright, blushing, and notice Adam doesn't turn; he continues supping a pint at the bar with his back to me. I pull up a stool and flatten my creased set-list at my feet. I toy with the mic and try to catch Charlotte's attention. She had promised to sing with me on the first track to ease me in, but she doesn't leave Adam's side as he nurses his pint. Clearly they have serious interview business to attend to. I see two girls from school at the back end of the room and one of them has the red face of someone who's been hysterically laughing.

An icy feeling starts to take hold. I catch the barman's eye, intending to tell him I can't sing tonight, but thinking I am prompting him he walks up to the stage, seizes the microphone and says, "We have a real treat for you tonight, ladies and gentleman. Emma Imrie, lead chanteuse of the recently signed London band Cherub, is performing a selection of her hits tonight for your delight and delectation."

His tone has teetered on the thin ledge of irony and praise that the English exist on. At the bar, I see Adam put his head down. The girls at the back of the room laugh loudly. Saskia whoops, but the sound is solitary, and its enhanced by the muting of the background music. The barman leaves me to enjoy the silence. "Hello everyone," I say. My voice booms around the room. "I Don't have any hits…" I begin.

"Or tits!" shouts the BMX kid at the door.

"But I see we have no shortage of pricks," I shoot back

An older couple, sharing a basket of fries, jump. I realise my remonstration has been too severe. The lady calls the barman over. I steel myself as I begin to strum some chords. The guitar sounds raw and I forget the chord sequence. When I apologise into the mike, the volume on my voice is so high that it makes everyone jump again. When I start wailing the first verse of "Doll Parts" I prove I am a long way from being a chanteuse. Another couple, who I recognise from one of Mum's dinner parties, get up to leave. They don't look at me. As I sing the woman stands next to Adam, who is hunching more and more. She remonstrates to the barman. I hear the phrase, "Tone-deaf" filter back to me.

As I plough through the song, Adam seems to tense even more. His expression is mirrored in Charlotte's face, and it is not good. It suggests that they have agreed that they have a shared take on music that I simply don't get, and furthermore that my performance is confirming that, all of which will make their inevitable love affair more awkward. I notice his pint glass is already drained.

The song ends to the sound of four hands clapping. I realise that the only applause has been from the girls at the back, and it was so slow that it revealed sarcasm. I feel so alone. Something cold seems to swim in my stomach.

"I'd like to invite my good friend Charlotte up to the stage to join me for this number," I say, my voice booming around the room.

Charlotte is talking to Adam. She doesn't turn to me when I say her name. I try to turn this into a joke. "My faithful friend, Charlotte," I say with a smirk, hoping that my voice will silence the hubbub. But people just look at me in irritation. Saskia, also keen to be alone with Adam, prods Charlotte. Charlotte doesn't turn to look at me, but shakes her head as she looks at the floor.

"I'll just soldier on alone then," I say with a lame laugh. But no one is listening and so I just start playing Hairy Food instead.

I am pouring my heart out about general body horror whilst people chatter through my set. Charlotte is laughing uproariously at everything Adam says. I finish the song, and there is no applause. My worst nightmare is playing out and I have a front row seat. Shouldn't this be my moment of glory? I try to work out how to tune my guitar, wondering if that is the problem, when the music comes on through the PA. I can feel my cheeks burning as the barman comes over. "Can we say one more and then you call it a night?" he asks.

I feel like ice cold water has been poured over my head. Something is swimming in my stomach, and I feel acidic and bloated. "But didn't we say half an hour?" I ask, forcing a smile onto my face.

"Well, I don't think it's quite what some of the regulars had in mind, Emma," he says, wincing, as he wipes his hand on his apron. He shakes his head. "We'll still pay you, but this will have to be the last one." He looks at the door with despair as another couple leave.

Adam has clearly caught these words, as he turns and looks at me with a bashful smile. I start to play the final song, Charlotte looking at me and mouthing the word, "Sorry." I shake my head at her. Anger infects my words and my playing. Adam starts to take an interest.

One of the older women shouts, "Give it a rest," as she goes to the bathroom. When the song finishes, no one claps. Adam taps at his pint for the barmaid. I get off the bar stool and lay my guitar down. It hums in protest at its unused voice.

From the back of the room, one of the girls shouts, "Top Of The Pops!" and all her friends laugh. I stand up, put my hands in my pockets, go over to the bathroom. The girl in the mirror looks fat and talentless. In the cubicle I flush the chain and during the noise from the flushing I stick my fingers down my throat. But then I remind myself that me being bulimic is what the patriarchy would want, and so I stop.

Afterwards we sit on the white sand at the edge of the harbour, watching the water slip out into the ocean. The sun is a spindly gold star in the corner of my right eye. My eyelashes break it into strands. We pass around a can of Red Stripe. It tastes like summer; warm, bubbly, heady. Adam is tapping ash into an empty can by his side. At one point he rubs the back of my hand. I feel so hollow. Whatever strange, creative substance I brewed within me to try and fill the hole has been drained away. I focus on the bobbing yachts on the white-blue water, on the clink of the boat rigging. I tell myself this place is too picturesque for misery.

"How do you think it went?" Adam asks, as Saskia and Charlotte paint each other's nails. They haven't said a word about the gig or looked at me since it. Their bodies are angular and unyielding, beautiful as church steeples. My wince offers Adam my response, but his expression remains impassive. He is pretending to be surprised by my reaction.

Saskia looks at me. A hundred deft calculations take place in her eyes. She realises, with the quickness only young women have, that she has to now say something kind but she's comforting herself that at least she can say it cruelly.

"You were great," she says. There is an earringless hole in her ear, which looks absurd given how she's throwing me about.

"Yeah," Charlotte echoes. "I would have joined you onstage but what if I end up reviewing you?"

This double blow of this cruelty is clever enough to be clearly planned, and all about her jealousy regarding Adam and I. She never floated the idea of reviewing the gig before it went badly, and it has also given her a reason for refusing to support me in favour of cosying up to my boyfriend. I shake my head, cursing that I didn't anticipate this move.

Charlotte and Saskia both smell like sun cream, like afternoons spent trying to bring yourself off and failing to get anywhere. There is a heavy, hormonal cloud around us. It feels like getting on the bus when the whole school is on it. I picture Adam having sex with all three of us in some room with the shutters down. The mole on Saskia's breast as she takes off her bra. The downy hair on Charlotte's arm illuminating as she loops her arm around my boyfriend's shoulders.

I can't bring myself to respond to either of them. I know how I look, all blocked up with secrets and resentment, like a big fat book no one dares to pull off the shelf. I kind of like the feeling; it's important and womanly. I wonder if, after twenty more years of it, I will evoke the sense of dread that my mother is expert at creating in people when she walks into a room, the feeling that she needs to be carefully handled and unpacked.

"At least I got paid," I say to Adam, but more for Charlotte. "Perhaps it just wasn't for them."

"Yeah," he says. "They just want to hear The Beatles or whatever."

Adam doesn't have the strength to unpack a real woman. He is still surprised that something happened in his career and now he gets to hang out with the opposite sex.

Charlotte and Saskia start leaning into each other and whispering. They'll both be ugly in a few years, I think, comforting myself. All the ancestral inbreeding will start to show in a general air of horsiness. They don't have the cultivated detachedness that real public-school girls use to protect themselves. The only girl I know who might be genuinely beautiful one day is Ruth. One day her frame will be strong enough to carry those heavy breasts, and she'll be confident enough to force stupid men to listen to her clever thoughts.

Girls like me and Ruth will get momentum and be on stages while they'll be all twenty-eight and pregnant by crap local men with zero ideas.

"It's a bit embarrassing," I whisper. "It was like I was being dismantled."

He nods, scrutinises my expression but doesn't reply. He looks out at the water and squints. He has saved all his pity for himself. He likes it when I fail. It makes him hate women less.

I follow his eyes. The shimmer on the ocean thickens, making it appear like a thick white bar is building on top of the waves. I close my eyes. I imagine the white-gold globe in the sun taking me inside it.

That night I dreamt about waves. In my morning slumber I finally understood Emma's first diary entry. It felt like the sea was calling me as well now. It was a feeling I knew I wouldn't have had if I hadn't spent so long thinking about Emma and walking on beaches, but it was an emotion that was becoming relentless. I was just wondering if I could be bothered to get up and close the blinding crack of gold light through the blinds when the door opened.

Ruth was standing there in rose-patterned pyjama bottoms and a faded blue t-shirt, her dark hair askew. "What's up?" I groaned, wondering if I was dreaming.

She moved over to the bed and lifted up the blanket. "River's on his paper round. I can't sleep. I'm too cold. Can I get in?"

"Yeah."

As she backed into me, her hair smelled like girl-conditioner and coco butter. I felt a sharp sensation of arousal as she skewered her backside into my hips. "Put your arm over me, warm me up," she said, pulling my limb over her shoulder.

Her proximity, her feminine scent, the pliant feel of her warm flesh, all felt so exciting that I decided I had to be dreaming. I hadn't done anything to deserve feeling close to a girl. "I heard you talking in your sleep," she murmured. "You do it all the time. I wanted to see if you were okay."

"Thanks," I said, wondering if she was going to object at the slight rubbing of my thumb on the back of her hand. Her little murmur told me she wasn't going to. But this high wire act of intimacy, in which the natural could at any moment be misconstrued, was erotic and exposing.

"I won't take too much notice of anything you say to me while we're cuddled up," she whispered. "I'll just assume you're dreaming."

I couldn't see her expression, to tell if she was being serious.

I curled up tighter against her. Part of me just wanted us to rub our clothes off and clasp against each other. Another part of me actually just wanted to cry in her arms. Her murmuring told me, almost theatrically, that she was slipping into her own dreams. I huddled tighter up against her and in that delicious slide back into sleep I decided that I would tell the truth. I wanted it out of me, and she had given me an excuse.

"I think you're so gorgeous," I whispered.

She murmured, half 'that's nice', and half 'please shut up'.

"I think you're the most beautiful woman I've ever seen," I

110

whispered, nuzzling into her hair. It hurt to say things that I meant so much.

She reached behind my head and pushed it deeper into her hair. "Aw. You're just hoping I'll let you put that thing inside me," she murmured.

"That's true. And also, I think I love you," I said, as I toppled backwards, wonderfully, into sleep.

Chapter Eighteen

When I woke up that morning Ruth was gone, but her scent on the pillow told me that all that had been real, that I hadn't dreamt it.

I kept telling myself that whatever I had said to her she had seemed to like, and at least she would put it down to me talking in my sleep anyway. But I still just couldn't face the thought of her seeing me in the kitchen and saying, in front of River, that I'd told her I thought I loved her.

With that, and the thought of what Emma had just told me, I realised I had to be on my own for a while. When River came back from his paper round, throwing fresh porn on the kitchen table like groceries (along with a packet of Rothmans), I told him was going to crash on the beach for a bit. I felt acutely aware of Ruth's movements upstairs.

"Why?" River asked. "Have you had a wet dream or something? Because I'd get them too, if I stopped wanking."

"No, it's not that."

Something was stopping me from going upstairs to tell Ruth that I was going. I knew it wasn't right to leave her without saying why. I even knew that I'd regret it. But I just didn't have the words to describe what I was feeling, let alone tell her it.

I decided to pack up my rucksack and take a pilgrimage to the spot on the beach where Emma had sat that night, after her gig. Something also told me that I needed to be alone, more alone than I had ever been, when I read the next pages of her diary.

I wondered if the spot I went to was where she had gone during the morning she had described in her first diary entry. I wondered if the sea would turn up and speak to me as it had done to her. I looked out at the water, thinking it all over. Struggling with the brutal truth that no one really wanted me.

It was strange being in a place that was so beautiful when you felt like that. I wondered if the setting should, by rights, have made me feel better, but instead it just made me feel wretched because I was unable to break through these feelings. I decided that pushing your way into situations that scare you is sometimes the only way to feel alive. That it's the only way to overcome that sense of blankness life often has, that sense that things will never improve. I hoped Emma realised that scaring ourselves is essential. I hoped she realised it was better to do a gig that went badly than to never try at all.

It occurred to me, sitting there, looking out at the white sun, how strange it was that Emma had described herself as 'dismantled'. Is that what she was, when she was lying in the coffin at the other end of the church?

I ran sand through my fingers. I wondered if enough sea would wash that image out of my mind and whether I'd ever see something else when I closed my eyes at night. I thought about how, when someone destroys themselves, you're left with such an ache that you can't do anything with. You want to go looking for that person to try and communicate with them. You go to places they were, as if hoping they'll be there in some way.

Maybe that's what all the walking was about that summer. The walking carried on in the days that followed. This incessant pacing around the coastline, day after day, as the sun beat down, turning me a deeper and deeper shade of brown. I had this vague idea that Emma was out there somewhere, that I could find her if I walked far enough, that she'd be throwing stones on some pontoon somewhere and I'd sit down next to her and she'd look up at me apologetically, like she'd merely taken something too far, and then all this would be over. There had to be somewhere I could go so that all this was over.

But I knew that even if I could find the path she'd been on, I could only take it so far. All I could do was get to that point in it where her footprints were last seen, and then look in the same direction as she had. That summer gave me the chance to do that. It was like I was under a spell. You can't get into someone else's state of mind, except with a lot of space. People would've said, "He's living on the beach because he's lost it over Emma dying." Ruth would have said, "He's just embarrassed because he told me he loved me." I think that's all sadly true, but I also think there was more to it than that.

There's this place where the harbour meets the village. Not many holidaymakers go there. It's just before all the huge mansions overlooking the sea. Above the beach is a belt of thick and tangled greenery. I slept in that dense undergrowth. Through it you could just about see the ocean.

On that first night I found the white-flecked black water terrifying. But the air was warm, and as the night went on, the sound of the sea was comforting. It became like a kind of family member, one that comforted you, but one who you couldn't get away from. It didn't speak to me like it had to Emma, but that was okay. It was there for me. I felt it in every atom of my being.

On that first night I could see through the trees columns of smoke from distant bonfire parties. The sound of distant laughter and of bottles being clinked while people had fun. It made me feel pretty lonely, knowing that I hadn't been invited to anything, and I was only at River's because my mum had asked them to take me on. It was awful, knowing that out there, people were falling in love, and holding hands, and having fun. I told girls I loved them moments after they cuddled me, and now I only had the incessant sound of the sea to keep me company. It barged its way in and then slipped back out and it didn't care who it touched.

That night I had all these dreams of being drowned, of my few belongings floating out on the Solent. I had wrapped them in plastic bags, but they never felt secure. I buried them in the sand and slept on them and they indented themselves in my body.

Five hours later I realised I had slept; my body having fitted into the contours of this bank. It was the mosquito bites that woke me up, and the sunlight beaming onto me as it filtered through the trees overhead. It felt obscene to be awake that early, knowing everyone else was lying all snug in their clean sheets.

The morning had an almost hallucinogenic feel about it. The web of light overhead, strands of it fusing and breaking. I realised a lie-in would be impossible. The sunlight would keep forcing my eyes to stay open. It was as if it was forcing me to be a part of nature.

I got up, and worked out what to swim in. I stashed my stuff under a rock; somewhere no dog or passing thief could see. I stepped out of the copse, my feet getting cut on pebbles as I trod my way down the pebbles to the water in my boxers. I was relieved to see that the tide was in. I dipped my feet in the sea and when I realised I had nothing to lose, I threw myself into the surf.

When I emerged, dripping, the sunlight started drying me. I had never felt cleaner, and fresher. It was like I'd been baptised.

As my mind hadn't been pinned by any human interactions, it started going to places so vivid and abstract that it was as if I was tripping. I realised that my mind was like a boulder, huge and rolling, and when the memory of some psychedelic dance track bubbled up, I found myself orchestrating music with my hands. My imagination skipped and skittered. The sand and the rocks and the waves had become playgrounds for my mind to play with.

I wondered if other people had ever felt such clarity about how reality can be twisted and altered. I doubted it, and the white heat of that thought invigorated me.

I made my way back to my stuff, and the awkward bit began. Having dried my hair and body on the towel, I had to start the walk; a mile-long trek to the holiday park where I would brush my teeth in the communal bathroom before the proper holidaymakers got there and crowded it up with their stinking, sweating bodies. In those bathrooms, all verruca floors and abandoned towels, I tried to smarten myself up a bit. As I brushed my teeth, I heard a man belching outside, like he was trying to empty his stomach.

I went into the village, to the Happy Shopper (which I was

not). I bought chocolate croissants and sprinkle doughnuts and flicked through copies of Melody Maker, NME and Deluxe. I read that someone had started a band called 'Aleka', the name I wanted us to use. Fate seemed to be taunting me with the consequences of wasting away on the margins. I remembered that, all over the world, people were bringing their ambitions to the fore. I quietened my sense of resentment by trying to persuade myself that one day this time might prove to have been deeply useful.

Feeling the newsagent's eyes on me, and smelling the growing scent of his cigar smoke, I quickly read reviews of The Chemical Brothers performing at somewhere called The Heavenly Social. It was a title that captured what I expected those venues to be. The review talked of "Spasmodic ravers, gurning as their ears are drilled by sirens, beats and psychedelia until derangement sets in." I gripped the pages and read of how the reviewer, "takes a zombie step, looks up at the DJ and realises that they are playing with a Mobius Strip of time." I had no idea what they were on about. But I knew that those lines were postcards from where life was really happening. I couldn't even afford the indulgence of buying the weeklies, which made their words all the more potent.

At the village bakery, I bought a coffee and realised how getting ready was starting to take over the whole day, and that this was probably why people got houses in the first place. As I ate my doughnuts and sipped my coffee on a bench in the centre of the village, I asked myself, what makes up a human life? Are you not human if you lack a proper bed and a job and a purpose? Do you need someone saying they love you back, in order to be human? Do you need to see them every day? And if the answer to all these things was yes, then why had I never felt more human? And if not, then why did people insist that you needed all those things?

I made my way back down to the beach and began starting to get really immersed. Everything had been leading up to when I would read her diary. I needed perfect seclusion to feel I was close to her. I needed the thick canopy of leaves above me and the soil of the bank under my feet. In a spot so dark that even sunlight could barely reach me. I needed to read a bit of this Courtney Love paperback biography that she took everywhere with her. I had this whole routine.

Reading those reviews makes me think of the one Emma got in Melody Maker, the review that changed so much for her back when she was the one making others wish they'd get out there and do it. It's in the diary of course, sellotaped to the back cover. Unfolding it in the heavy shade made me realise I almost knew it off by heart. It was like a prayer, readying me for the meditation ahead.

Grunge gets a new outfit
Cherub
Purple Turtle, London

Francesca Stefani
August 30th 1999
Roll up, roll up. This is the era when the coveted accessory is Madonna's latest yoga pose and some rudimentary knowledge of The Kabbalah. Then what are Cherub thinking of, pulling on the baby-doll dresses of Courtney Love? Isn't that all so passé, darling?

Well, no. Tonight grunge, Riot grrrl, whatever the hell you call it, is getting more than new boots. It's getting a bloody hard kicking. Clockwork Orange, underpass style.

While most of Cherub's pals will be swotting up on their new university syllabus, these four girls from the arse end of nowhere (no really, some are from The Isle of Wight) are bringing an art-rock freshness to a genre badly in need of it.

"I thought London was supposed to be sexy," says vocalist Emma Imrie, before the band launch into scorching next single 'Namedropper'. "But all the men here look like they need a bloody good wash."

It's not an untypical statement from the brash, quixotic frontwoman, and what's surprising is the warmth with which it's received. Whilst the London crowd try to work out which haircut they all should get and decide on having three at once, Imrie goes from visibly shaking to wilfully staring the crowd

117

out by the shows end. And all this 'character' only seems to charm them. Even though, as a musician her fingers are still finding their place on the fretboard, her songs offer some sharp new ideas. 'Hairy Food' bizarrely adopts the worldview of a bulimic teenager being cajoled to finish her porridge, creating a kind of Grunge Goldilocks for the late twentieth century.

Then there's Imrie's voice. One minute Lolita-like, and the next a terrifying caterwaul that suggests the arrival of a banshee in shining Mary Janes. The serrated riffs and menacing drums add a plentiful sense of theatre. The angelic backing vocals and angular basslines suggest the impending album will contain a breadth of textures. But at the centre of all this early-stages noise is a piercing new perspective. Check out new song 'The Sculptress', with its dark asides about Princess Diana and Kinderwhore. Could Kenickie pen something as sharp as that?

Cherub make songs for heartbroken girls who want more from life than to watch their boyfriend's boring indie band whilst pretending to be impressed. But what makes them genuinely intriguing is the acute sense of pain that seems to drive Imrie. "This song is for any girl brought up to believe boys do everything better than us. In other words, it's a song for everyone in the front row," she says, prompting cheers from all the glitter pusses.

Emma Imrie is a suicide blonde who looks like all of Elastica combined and whose voice has more than a touch of Courtney Love. And if that quote is enough to make the record companies come-a-running, then perhaps there is some justice in this world. Screw the ratings system. It's five stars from me.

It was only after all that reading preparation that I could read the next pages of her diary. Knowing that the time I was spending in my sister's company was fast running out. Knowing that the slenderness of the remaining pages, and the greedy size of the drawings between each entry meant I had only a few more situations left in which my sister was still alive.

The fact that the next sequence started with the word

'Adam' left a sinking feeling in my stomach. The fact was, for all the vague statements made about how she died, the truth about what happened was coming. It was coming any sentence now.

Chapter Nineteen

Adam has told me he'll probably be in The Ship, and I've often wondered how he can spend so long sat nursing a pint in a boozer when he could be writing. How is his band going to improve unless he works at it, unless he even joins them in the studio? As I walk to him, I wonder what I'd actually do to be in his position.

But on arrival I can see why he is not writing. His eyes are like pissholes in the snow. The pupils are black and dilated. He shrinks and cowers in the corner under the window.

"Emma," he says, as if greeting a doctor that has come to give him an injection.

It feels so horrible to see him like this, after all Mum said. I moved to London, yes, to make it, but also for him, to build a relationship. He was constantly lingering around me at London gigs, ensuring no other man spoke to me, interrupting conversations I had with anyone. We would go outside and have deeply intense exchanges about 'what we'll do'. Then when I bit the bullet, defied Mum and made the trip, he began to retreat into himself.

I have told Aunt Carol about this on the proviso she will not tell Mum. It seems a big ask, given that the next time they fall out she'll love to have something on Mum, so I know it's only a matter of time until she uses this info. Mum only has to push the right buttons. But in fairness, my auntie had two bits of genuine advice. One was, 'Hurt people hurt people', which I don't understand. Why would hurt people hurt people? Especially if they have someone loving them. And she also said, 'Broken people crave things they think they can't have because it gives them something to pin their hopelessness on. But if they get what they thought they couldn't have they resent it as they realise it was not the key to their happiness'. This made a bit more sense. But I have refused to believe that is what is happening here. I love Adam, even when I hate him. and will do anything for us.

With all the things that I've said, I've never seen his eyes like this before.

"Christ, are you okay?" I ask, standing over him.

He looks past me, but as he smiles, his jaw unhinges in a way that makes my skin crawl. I get the distinct feeling something has snapped inside him and is now swinging away in there. The hand he places on the table is white to the point of translucency. "Rough few days," he sighs. From his dry lips I can smell vodka, alcopops and cigarettes.

He swings his skeletal head to my direction. I realise that all those metaphors about mutilation and tragic death were more than just cosmetic. They were postcards from the brink. And 'the brink' is not an exciting, edgy place. It's a place where people fall off. I realise that all the signs were there, but I mistook them for rock 'n roll.

"How was the meeting?" he asks, cradling his glass.

"Humiliating," I answer, as I sit down next to him.

He smiles, with what seems genuine happiness.

"Adam, that's not a good thing," I say.

He cocks his head. "No. But it is an unsurprising thing."

As I plan my counter claim I look around. The pub, I realise, is actually homely. There are piles of board games in wardrobes. Vintage framed pictures, gilt-stained windows. Is his residency here an attempt to feel he is part of a warmer world? He has poisoned this corner, at the very least, and the lingering look from the barman suggests he thinks so too.

"This guy," I start. "He calls me in because he says the label is interested in a girl band and then he spends the whole time dismissing me for being a woman."

He laughs. "I knew he'd be like that."

"So why didn't you warn me?"

His smile is blank. I detect that any sense of shame he has is a shard of glass, buried deep in his various issues.

"I thought it was obvious." He exhales and looks down. "I

suppose I thought you were smart."

"I am. Adam, that's mean. Why are you being so mean?"

He shrugs.

In an icy moment Adam makes sense. The person that took polaroid's of every woman he slept with was never going to have goodness running through him like a stick of Brighton Rock.

*He is made of wounds, I think. His body is a place that binds all these wounds together. He is made of hurt and confusion. That's why he does what he does, the messed-up music and the promiscuity and the solitary drinking. Not because he's unconventional, but because he can't handle **life**.*

I have a moment of revelation. If he can't care for himself, how can he ever care for me?

I look at him and know that pity and disappointment is scored across my eyes.

"Get us a pint, Emma?"

He pulls a cigarette out.

"Maybe you should go easy on them," I say, noticing his packet is almost empty.

He fans his hands in a way that reminds me of Bowie on the cover of 'Heroes'. "Okay, Mum," he says. He clearly considers the retort insufficient. "Why?" he asks.

As I move to the bar, I decide that he never used this tone before I moved to London. Not once.

A glance over, as the pints are poured, sends a lattice of cold spreading across my shoulders. I have never seen those marks on his arm before.

"Finally," he says, wrapping a claw round the pint.

"Adam, what the fuck is that on your arm?"

He is wearing a t-shirt and has made no effort to cover them up. He offers the same smile he did when I told him about the record exec.

"You're not using, are you?"

He pulls the pint to him. "Oh Jesus, Emma. Don't be so judgemental. It was a one-off. I'm under a lot of pressure." He looks at me. "You wouldn't understand."

I put my hand on his. "Adam, you can't be serious. That

122

sort of shit is beneath you."

He looks at the surface of the liquid. "In some situations, you have to do what you have to do. To fit in." He looks at me. "Anyone who's anyone dabbles."

Someone else's voice is inflecting his. Those are not his words. Who is he ventriloquizing?

"What?"

He looks at me. His blank expression, his lack of focus, his shrinking eyes. They make me feel ill. His mouth falls open. He threatens to laugh, but instead speaks.

"I'm nobody. Who are you? Are you nobody too?"

I feel sick. How he could he use that line against me?

Was Mum right?

I want to cry. Right there in the pub. Then that makes me feel even more like a stupid little girl, which is exactly what that fat executive wanted and exactly what my boyfriend now wants as well.

I bite my lip. I tell myself not to give in and humiliate myself in front of him.

I can almost feel myself developing new layers of skin over the one that has proved itself tissue thin.

I can't look at him. It is the most horrible feeling, realising that after all the arguing that your parents just don't get it, that in fact they might have 'got it' all too well.

I look at him and know I am pleading with my eyes.

He smiles at the sight of my tears. I am closer to being on his level, and that's what he wants.

"Perhaps you shouldn't judge a man unless you've walked in his shoes," he says.

It is at that moment that I know. It is a fact as plain as the marks on his arm and the weak sun in the window. Possibly today, possibly tomorrow, I am going to take heroin.

Hell and high water.

The sunlight was stinging my eyes now. I lay back on the soil and thought of how I never heard her use that phrase. It was so far from the sister I knew that it didn't belong in her mouth. It suggested some black angel taking her over, enclosing her in her wings. As I closed my eyes and lay down on the bank, a knot of pain pulsed at the side of my stomach. Was pain never-ending? Was that all there was? Even in my little retreat, where I had wrapped myself in leaves instead of cotton wool, the pain still got to me. And all I read about was pain. I wanted to lie in the dirt and let the soil take me. There really was no point in any of it now.

I told myself that at least I had those words. At least, for whatever dread they offered, I would have the chance to interpret something rather than just silence. It's the silence of the world that is really brutal, the silence of having nothing else to learn about her. No answers, no new experiences, no new songs. As the tide splashed up the bank and the sweat dried on my forehead, I had to accept that her next entry would most likely make for more difficult reading.

I rolled onto my stomach and prayed that the dog barking in the distance would stop. There are light moments in life, and there are dark moments, I thought. And I reminded myself that the dark moment I was about to enter would pass. Then I inhaled and started to absorb the last few pieces of Emma that I had left.

Chapter Twenty

I can see down the hallway that the living room is dark. As we pass adjoining rooms, Adam limply holds my hand. I can see people in the rooms, crashed out on mattresses. Are they drunk? I've never seen a naked woman on a naked mattress, and some of the men passing in and out of these doors don't look like the types to look out for a woman in that state.

The people in these rooms are in various levels of hell, I tell myself.

There is laughter echoing through this apartment and it has an unhinged edge to it. As we get to the entrance of the kitchen, a bearded man in a waistcoat, his thick arm muscles covered in tattoos, bars our way. "Woah," he says, toking on a spliff. "And you two are?"

"Marcus invited us," Adam says.

"For fuck's sake, let him in," says a whiny voice behind him. It takes me a moment to remember who that mewl belongs to-the singer from Ashtray Cult.

We step into the living room. Even in the gloom I recognise so many faces from bands I used to study in Melody Maker. People are sat on the floor round the coffee table and standing in a tight semi-circle by the window. They're stripped of their make-up, and the men aren't wearing their thin ties and sharp suits in here. One of the women from a band I've admired doesn't look up as we come in. My throat starts to tighten. Through the gloom, it appears as if she is trying to roll something. She curses, then pulls another corner off a swab of cotton wool and starts again, her lanky hair falling. Some of the women's lips look cut, and their eyes have dark rings. Is that the image now?

I look away look as Adam pulls up a cushion and takes his

125

place in the semi-circle. I try to work out if I can hear music playing. My mouth has never felt so dry. Something is churning in my stomach in an awful, stop-start rhythm.

Outside I can see the tiles of the station. I've passed Kings Cross so many times and never thought to look up here, at this window. Why would I? I had no idea what was going on in here. And who was doing it.

Adam tightens a brown belt around his arm. His under arm is a mass of twisting veins. He starts to rub one of them, near the crook of his elbow. He takes a cotton wool pad from the women and rubs it three times on the vein.

"You came to the right place," says a blonde bloke I recognise from pages of the NME. His band just got signed for a million pounds. His lopsided grin is in every weekly at the moment. I have read all the interviews with him. But he didn't mention this in any of them. He fiddles with a syringe, the muscles under his red Adidas t-shirt clenching, the light catching the blonde tips in his hair. Someone holds out a serving spoon for him, with carefulness. He presses the tip against the dark liquid on the spoon and draws the plunger up. He hands the syringe to Adam.

He gets up, moving to stand over me. I can smell sweat and sleep from his t-shirt, the smell of dried hair gel that has pressed against the same pillow for days. He is clamouring round me, as Adam takes the syringe off him and taps it, inspecting it. He is watching to make sure the bubbles are at the top of the liquid, teasing it to make sure there is no air in the syringe. I try to ignore him and don't look up to see if, through the dim light, he is leering at me. He looks around him. "My bowels are churning now," he says, to no one in particular. I can smell the pasties they sell at King's Cross on his breath.

He leans in, ensuring Adam takes a big hit. Then Adam is slumping back, and he misses the pillow. I realise they've been placed in a way to catch a certain kind of fall. He hits his head on the wall and slumps into a strange V-shape. I want to ask if he is alright, but something tells me I will be humiliated if I do.

The singer laughs.

The man at the door stands over us. Someone passes the singer a black belt.

"Yeah?"

I'm panicking. His fingers are squeezing my shoulder. I tell myself Adam is going to come to in a moment. Mum is surely going to burst in, turn the music off and pull open the curtains at any moment. Although I am sure, almost sure, all this is going to happen I don't protest as he takes my arm, twists it around, and finds a vein. The hair falls over my face. I don't want him to see my eyes.

The liquid in the vial looks dirty. I can smell tobacco, faeces. The room smells like burnt caramel. And all the laughing. So much laughing, and laughing that never completely stops. The needle pops the skin. I look around. All the activity. All the stasis.

This is where nothing happens, I tell myself.

He pulls the plunger up and I see a rosy cloud of my blood mix with the brown. The plunger is pushed. And then, I don't know what then. Nothing, for a moment. And then so much endless, flowing energy is pulsing through me. All the squalor and the fear has vanished. I am hunched over. The sweetest, most swinging sound is filling my ears. It seems ridiculous that I was ever anxious and scared. This feels so, so great. I feel as if I am looking down on my body, as if I'm a higher intelligence that can perfectly guide me with total ease.

"Not bad, right?" someone says.

It is all excitement and adrenalin, and there is more behind that, and more annexes of pure swinging bliss behind that. A pathetic word bubbles out of my mouth. I try to cling onto the feeling, to forage through it. I am sure I can find and work out so much through it. Through my blurred vision I see everyone gathering round, to see my reaction. Even the guy at the door looks over and grins. Some of the women narrow their eyes at me, and I want to tell them how cool they are, how beautiful I know they are, how glad I am to get to meet them. How special this feels. But in that moment, nothing really matters. I'm above it all. I just decide to collapse into the feeling. To not panic. For now there's no words, there's nothing.

All of the pain and all the problems have gone. And then, a retreat. The smells in the room come back. I can sense desperation in here, and fear. I can smell lice, sweat, vomit. More than I ever could before. I feel like an empty shell, horrified of the squalor of my existence. I remember that I was once a little girl talking to the ocean and the shame is so acute that I have to dismiss it so I don't cry.

But when I was high, there was no shame. Not then.

So now I knew. At the end of the day, the drugs weren't only about peer pressure. They were more about pain. Or, more accurately, her trying to get rid of pain.

Chapter Twenty-One

I closed my eyes and tried to stop the angry pulse of my heart. I was sure that if I didn't, it would burst out of my ribcage and I'd die, blood everywhere, bits of brain, pieces of young Jeff.

I remembered the phone call about Emma's first overdose. I remember every single moment of what happened. One after the other. That dark chill of a feeling.

Now was the time to face up to that day. To unpack what I'd previously boxed and kept up in some distant part of my own mental attic.

It was 9 am, and I was watching The Big Breakfast. It was half term and we were back in the rented house on the island. The trip had been well-timed, allowing River and I to watch the football at his house. Last night, even Ruth had joined us to scream at the screen, pretending we were adults who knew about sport. England had been knocked out by Romania, despite an Alan Shearer goal having just seen off Germany. I had woken up fostering a sense of unfairness, nursing the idea that life just didn't work out. I had no idea of the extent to which that feeling was going to be built upon that day.

I was bracing myself for Mum to come down and tell me to turn it off, for her to wail yet again that, 'It's for kids, Jeff'. But she didn't come and say that. She stayed on the phone. All I could hear from downstairs was sharp, motherly notes that made me tense up more and more.

I assumed Dad had done something unbelievable again. Threatening even the idea that the only thing he cared about was his sex life, and the excuses he needed to keep coming up with to ensure it kept him away from this house. But then I started to realise it was even worse than that. There was something bigger moving around the house. I thought of those big, black wings. Whenever I thought of Emma around that time, I had this really strong image of a beautiful woman with big black wings, coming to collect her.

Mum came downstairs, her face pale. In her dressing gown and rollers. "Turn that off," she said.

"What is it?"

"Emma."

'Emma' was a word often used to describe a multitude of sins, stinky messes, complex negotiations and fallouts. I was used to teasing out details, amongst the onslaught of Mum's rapidly accumulating despair. It was a game I hated playing. It was like pulling out blocks of Jenga and waiting for the whole stack to fall. I felt like Mum forced me to play the game and then the fallout when the blocks came down seemed like it was of my making. I knew there'd be a moment at which all the pain burst out of her, and that the moment I was dreading.

"What's happened?"

"It's that Adam. I *knew* he'd lead her astray."

"What did she do?"

"Drugs, Jeff. She took drugs." She flashed her hand up to her temple. "And because she's a stupid child who doesn't know what she's doing, it's…"

Her face crumpled. I jumped up and put my arm around her. "What?"

"She's had an overdose."

I remember the drive to London. The capital had never felt less glamorous, and whatever castles Emma had built in the sky around it had never felt so fanciful. That morning, London was a confusing combination of flecked rain on concrete, closed kebab shops, sad Muslims looking like they wanted to be somewhere else. London had a brutal, almost metallic edge to it. I remembered a phrase Donna once used when Emma said she was moving there. She said, "London's got a big, swinging dick. And at some point, it fucks everyone."

Looking out the window I asked myself if you could replace London with life, if London was life.

Now I understand what she meant. The hurt on people's faces. All the unresolved, flaring, spreading hurt. It made me think of those pictures of lungs that they showed us in biology. Tiny little branches leading to more tiny little branches. Branches of pain, that you couldn't erase. That just got finer the closer you looked. Pain made up of lies and bewilderment and sheer confusion.

I looked out of the window. I thought about the sense of menace oozing from the cracks. It was real, and it had a sense of inevitability about it. It all flowed one way. Down the drains, down to some buried, bubbling canal of pure black. I told myself that if I ever went down there and touched it, I would never be able to wash it off.

At traffic lights the indicator ticked, and Mum fumbled, angrily, for cigarettes. I could smell her morning breath in the hot air of the car. When she sparked up, she burnt her fingers and then threw the green plastic lighter across the dashboard. The cigarettes didn't calm her; they made her worse. "Oh, Emma," she kept saying, in various shades of despair, melancholy and anger. I had a feeling, one I could barely face, that there were a *lot* more conversations about Emma to come.

We swept up the grass-lined driveway to the hospital. As we went inside, I smelt the dank scent of overcooked vegetables in the long, winding corridors. The doorways we passed offered glimpses into wards which appeared to be pulsing with despair. Inside the wards I could see coughing patients, ridiculously thin and pale men, old women with their eyes closed. These women looked they were in a state of almost saintly pain. I thought of the nuns that scared me when I was a kid. These women were close to another place, a more serene place. They looked that way because they were readying themselves for it, I told myself.

After a tense chat with a Chinese nurse, Emma was found, sat in the window of an almost empty day care room.

"Oh, Emma," Mum sobbed, in a totally new voice. She ran over to the window. Emma winced as Mum kissed her head and pulled her slender body to her. "You really think boys are worth this?" she hissed, clasping Emma to her and looking out of the window. The corners of Mum's eyes were wet.

I held Emma's free hand, and, to my surprise, she let me,

131

although she didn't look up. Her hand was so pale and thin. She didn't say anything. She didn't even look at me. Something told me this was one of those moments when behind all the illusions and hope and lies you see someone for what they really are. Caught in the spiral of life. After a beat Emma's hand went to her brow. "Mum, he left me," she said, and she broke into a wrenching sob.

"Oh, baby," Mum said, holding her daughters head to her coat. She still hadn't unbuttoned it.

I had never felt so spare, so useless. I tried to work out what my granddad would do. "Can I get anyone a drink?" I whispered.

Mum's expression faltered and then resolved.

"Go get us two teas. And get yourself one," she said, nodding her head at the corridor. "There's three pounds in my purse."

Mum's handbag smelled of Parma Violets and dried foundation. As I found it, Emma started shaking and then she began crying. I could see the brown roots in her hair. I could see the small pink hearts on the hem of her knickers. Stripped of her cosmetics and bracelets and earrings, she looked very vulnerable. She was all scar tissue, and mum was trying to soothe it. "Oh baby. Baby, baby, baby," she said, as Emma started sobbing. "He's just a boy. He's not worth this. No one's worth this."

As I left the room, I heard Emma say, "He just phoned me and ended it." I looked back for a second. I could see snot shining around her nose, and the red around her eyes, the crazy framing of those wild, wide eyes with hair that was at once black, blonde and orange.

I had never seen her like this, but somehow, I'd always known this sort of thing was a part of who she was. So much of Emma circled situations like these. I tried to deny the truth that we all have times when we become children, when it all falls apart. I promised myself I wouldn't ever believe what a girl promised me; no matter how much my body made me feel like I was in love. I promised myself that I just wouldn't buy into it, and let love ruin me, like it had ruined her. I couldn't

132

believe I had to see my sister like this all because some guy wanted to have fun with her and because the whole thing now no longer worked for him. All because he refused to adjust. I told myself that he had chosen to do this to her rather than to feel what she felt.

When we took her to the car, Emma was wearing a coat Mum had brought from home that was too small for her. I wondered whether family members ever brought the right clothes to people in hospital.

Emma was kind of still in the backseat next to me for the start of the trip. But Mum's tense body language at the wheel betrayed something I already knew. A meltdown was coming.

I remember feeling incredulous at the realisation Adam hadn't visited her. It seemed to me like a judgment of him. Breakups are all understandable, but if someone's become sick as a result, surely the ex needs to step up if no one else is around. Are they really off the hook after a single phone call? Does that really mean that one phone call makes it as if the relationship never happened? I realised there was no judge or jury to compel or condemn him. There was just shitty behaviour, and the flaring, throbbing wound it left. He'd just go on with his life.

It seemed a brutal insight into how much this London crowd really cared for her. And I knew this was humiliating for Emma, given all her claims that the capital would be her new home, given that it was Mum and I who were there for the crying, the snot, and to fetch the tea. Always, in any crisis, sodding cups of tea, like they are some kind of magic elixir.

I started watching Emma out the corner of my eye. I didn't appreciate at that age the different way women loved, using their bodies and their heart and their spirit and their soul. I didn't appreciate that they felt part of someone when they were in love with them. I promised myself I would never tell a woman I loved them unless I simply couldn't bear not to. I told myself that relationships were not a game, no matter much everyone wants you to join in.

So even during this awful moment, Emma was teaching me.

That was the moment I realised that when someone breaks

your heart, every moment is agony. If they've done it in a cowardly way, or if you've got desperate and sick as a result, there's all the pain and humiliation that comes with people knowing that as well. It's so bad that you just don't want to be in your own body anymore. You're done, expired. Other people have to prop you up for a few steps and the hope is that at some point you'll walk by yourself again. And that brings you even lower because you have to admit that you've failed so much that you need to be carried. But what if you can't walk any more on your own?

Emma couldn't even speak during that journey. Once she opened her mouth, she started crying and couldn't stop. It all came out like a torrent. I thought that the dark river under the city was coming through her. It was like waiting for rain to fall, almost a relief to see it come out, but it was so scary. She was shaking. She banged her head on the window. She tore at her hair. "Okay baby. Calm down," Mum would say, and then her tone would totally change. "For God's sake, Jeff," she would hiss. "Hold your sister's hand." And I would, but it was like trying to hold onto dead leaves.

Mum went between hunching over the wheel and then springing back as she tried to calm her, as if she was most scared of all that Emma would stop hearing her.

It's weird because in the future, when Emma's records got re-released, people would keep going on about how special my family was. But at moments like that it felt like the opposite was true. I didn't know that things like this happened in loads of families. I thought this was a shameful secret that showed how crazy we were.

"Where can we pull over? "Mum asked me, gripping the wheel. The pressure was building in my head. I could feel it careering around my ears. In the end I hissed, "*Where the hell is Dad?*" Mum's eyes flashed at me in the mirror. "You know where he is. And you know who he's with. Give it a rest. We're on our own," she said, glancing over Emma. "It's just the three of us."

Whatever happened to 'the three of us?' When did it become 'the two of us'?

I was learning so many things about people that morning, about what they were really made of, about what happened when their bullshit got exposed. But I felt like everything I was learning about people was bad. People were cowards. People were unable to do what they said they'd do, but these disgusting messes wouldn't stop them from making the same promises in the future. I knew they'd carry on doing that despite all the mess because, in any given moment, all they want is to not feel so alone. They just keep promising you everything, trying to stave off the second they're left on their own with it all. They just keep doing it, people. They do.

Adam had promised Emma everything and, of course, she had believed him. She wasn't messed up at the time.

She was now.

From my reverie on the bank, I looked back at the strange, dark shape of Mum at the wheel, scanning the rain, scanning a listless and unconcerned London. Me looking for a service station and Emma crying and tearing at her hair in the backseat, and I think one thing. Why did no one work out that Emma was going to do it again?

Why did no one work out that there was only one way to block out the pain, and now Emma knew about it at some point she'd return to it, and that, in future, she'd use that thing even more than she had done before?

I hung in all those memories, in a sun-kissed reverie. I was half awake, half asleep, half dead, half alive.

Emma chose to make her life a truncated limb, a snubbed-out nerve ending. I prefer to keep the nerve of my life flaring. Wide open.

I stared up at the sky and refused to blink until it gave me answers. I tried not to think that in every way Emma was gone.

Except for one last entry. An entry, I knew, that must've been written in the very place she died.

It'd be the closest I'd get to her now.

Chapter Twenty-Two

I remember when all I wanted was to be included, when I would have done anything for opportunities like this. So I'd be damned if Adam's cowardly phone call was going to make me forget the opportunities I'd earned for myself.

Hospital was humiliating. It was scary to find out how quickly you can unravel. I know I took it too far and, at some point, I will need to figure out why I did that. Sometimes you get in a frame of mind and it has to crash for you to properly reset. That's what I am trying to do. Reset. You have a chance to start a new life after a crash like that.

I dyed my hair white blonde in the sink. When I looked in the mirror the expression of the girl looking back at me made me want to cry. But with my new hair, I decided nothing bad could ever happen to me now, so I wiped the tears away.

Perhaps you can't learn some things right away. Perhaps they take time. But I have some sense of what the first step on my new journey will be. I drag myself back to London and try to ignore the fact that I am finding each breath pretty painful. But I need to try and collect whatever strands of a life I still have there, to try and reclaim what I have started.

My mum begs me not to come back to this city. She tells me that she has this really bad feeling, that she doesn't think it's safe. She insists that I take a friend, but I am loathe to admit there isn't one who'll do the job. Donna briefly agrees but then has to bail. So I go alone, and Mum knows she can't really stop me. It is my life.

In a pub near Camden Lock, I nurse a pint at the bar. Sitting there with a full face of makeup, the spots of rouge on my face betraying too long spent getting ready. Coupled with the white Alice band and the brown fur coat, I look a bit like a doll. Businessmen come in and wonder if I am fresh meat. I remember that however shitty I feel, I have developed all this power over men, and now is the time to start using it. There is some serious situation-cleaving to do.

The inevitable indie sleazes in long shoes come in and I don't even have to properly smile at them before they start chatting me up. Men can sense an opportunity. Anything flapping about on the floor that smells vaguely female and they're there. A couple of forced laughs later and I am part of whatever dreadful trajectory they want their night to take.

One of the women overlooking her under-talented charges is called Tracy, and she seems all right. Her band chat about the fact that the Ashtray Cult crowd, led by some guy called James, are hosting a party in some run-down house outside the city. Hertfordshire? These scuzzy types make out they are such men of the people, and they only bring up the huge stately homes their families live when it suits them. I suspect Adam will be there and so I say to Tracy, "What do you think?"

She shrugs and says, "Why not?"

"When one person lets you down, you have to move onto the next idea," I say, thinking of Donna's advice.

"What?" she asks.

"Nothing," I answer.

The thing is, I know how breakup politics work. The battle lines are being redrawn, and if I'm not careful, Adam will label me as 'crazy' and no-one on the scene will work with me. But if I re-enter the fray as soon as possible and people see me as a non-negotiable presence, I might have some kind of an afterlife in Camden. So I get in the car and we drive through the drizzle to somewhere called Tring.

In my fur coat I am hot, and the ribbons of white fabric that make up my dress stick to me. There is the fug of alcohol-breath in the car. Cramped up against Tracy's parka in the backseat, we listen to demos of bands that I know will be bigger than mine, with songs that make me feel hollow. I realise I must've missed something in them, and that makes me feel stupid

I know what James' crowd will be like. Vince has been

spouting off in Ashtray Cult interviews about 'chasing the dragon' and 'the brown stuff', and there's this video on the Rosary forums (I know, I should lay off it) of Vince and Adam in some kind of manic state, painting on pristine white walls with what looks like blood. Adam must know Vince is trying to screw him. But why Adam finds those sorts of people worth his time is beyond me.

Me, Tracy, and what looks like some male hairdressers in women's leather jackets park up outside a run-down stately home with lights on in its upper windows. We enter by walking between pillars. For a moment, I fancy that I'm in an Evelyn Waugh novel. The fur coat helps. I suspect that any men at this party will pounce on me, the over made up girl with the air of vulnerability. I decide to play up to it.

The massive front door has been left open. I suppose when you have all this money, it means nothing to you. I enter with contempt, which is the way everyone seems to enter new places in this scene. But my disdain simply doesn't run deep enough. In a ruined dining room, Vince and the rest of Ashtray Cult are listening to some torturous Throbbing Gristle record while they pass around a bong. There is something else mixed in the low cloud that hangs around the tattered chandelier and it makes my head throb. The air is so thick, and the men are so stoned, that they barely see me. I must appear like a cartoon character.

I sit on the floor next to Tracy, at Vince's feet. I watch his band laugh hysterically at everything the sprawling Vince imparts to us from his leather throne. So far, no one has even looked at me. The energy of the room comes from Vince, and it is homo erotic. Girls are party spoilers, and my power has been muted. I find myself saying to Vince, from my place in his Greek Chorus, "I thought you were playing in Thailand."

He looks up at me. With the air of someone speaking with incredible generosity to an impertinent stranger he says, "April."

We both know I am looking for Adam, and the bite I feel when I realise he isn't here is savage. And even though I look desperate, who can really blame me? Who would really be satisfied with a single phone call ending a big relationship? Of course, I am hoping to pick up the stray ends.

A Korean guy, looking up from his bong says, "Weren't you Adam's girlfriend?"

"Girlfriend is a strong word," Vince says, and when everyone cackles, I just want to die.

I feel Tracy studying my reaction. She's already worked the whole situation out.

"What do you mean?" I ask.

Vince smirks, and leans back. A fat, bearded guy in a waistcoat bends over him. "I thought he was going out with that woman who was on the front of that porno, Club Magazine," he says. "The one who looks like Jennifer Aniston."

"Yeah, he is," Vince says, and I feel the blood drain from my face. I try to find the will to smile, but I realise I have no energy. Humiliation has utterly drained me. It makes the back of my head tingle. The blank looks around me indicate that the subject is now closed.

It's clear no-one wants me here. My cover has been blown and I am now trapped in the scene where I have been shown up. I now have to pretend I like these people, which will then make me feel even worse. I even force a smile at Vince's remark, as if I am somehow in on the joke. "Come on, girl," Tracy says. "Let's find some beer."

She and I don't even look for a kitchen. We just search for a decent place to sleep for the night. I can only hope that this flaring feeling will have faded by the morning after some kip. Rock bottom, and underneath that, various other rock bottoms you never knew about.

As we walk up the stairs, I see someone has written 'This Beautiful House Is Condemned' on the stairwell wall in red paint. At least, I hope it is red paint.

We find what was probably once a main bedroom, a four-poster bed with a mattress on it, still covered in its plastic. We decide that we'll sleep together on it, under some coats. Tracy is studying the view of the wet hills from the window when she says, "Christ." I ask what she's seen, and she points out a bundle of half-used burnt tin foil, along with a small brown box with dope inside. "At least if they're noisy we can block it out," she says. "If only we had some syringes."

I show her the purse full of fresh syringes that Adam gave me. "Right," she says.

I wish she hadn't shown me that box.

Any chance that she and I will stick together vanishes when we go downstairs, and some guy in a ponytail puts his arm around her and says, "I'm so happy you're here." They're soon necking on in the corner of the lounge, and when he starts hitting the pipe, Tracy joins in. I remember the way Adam did it, the way he taught me to do it, and I realise that these people are more serious about brown than he ever was. She waves at me to join in, and this really weird thing happens. A voice in my head screams the word, "No."

It is not my imagination, and at that point I am stone cold sober. It's like a metallic voice that's powerful enough to scare me. My heart races really fast and I look around, not believing no one else heard it.

It scares me so much that, for a few minutes, I stumble around the house, past the ruined cocktail bars in the corners of rooms enunciated by chandeliers, past the scarred mirrors that frame the wide-eyed women with the white shoulders and the white hair.

I go outside. The lights in the driveway blast on, insulting in their strength. I pick my way over the wet grass to what appears to be, through some trees, a lake. The rain in the grass creeps up my plastic heels until my rose-coloured tights get wet. My coat has fallen around my elbows, and my exposed shoulders become shivering gooseflesh. I stumble through a thin copse of trees, and slip down a muddy slope to where silver, freezing water is lapping up at sharp pebbles. I look back through the trees at the house. It is a distant bubble, shining and removed. I feel so drunk, so empty, that I am sure I won't make it back.

For a minute I think of throwing myself in the water, of being found tomorrow in the horrid morning light. I will look like a beautiful, pale Ophelia, weeds clinging to her slimy legs, one lost heel that is never recovered, all that wet white hair. I close my eyes and the image of my corpse is so clear that I wonder if there is a reason why I have so many pictures of Ophelia in my journal. Perhaps all this was destined.

That is when I go upstairs and end up here, lying on that mattress, looking out the bay window at the sheer darkness, trying not to imagine what has happened in this room.

I have found a few beers that I hope I can numb myself with. I know I might need something stronger, especially if I am to block out the noise and get some sleep. But is going downstairs such a good idea? Adam clearly isn't coming.

Sometimes you have to accept that the thing you've been waiting for simply isn't coming.

The temptation to stay in my little corner and watch the stars until morning comes is overwhelming.

The choice is between being with them or being left with myself.

And with a small smudge, that's where it ends, with my sister contemplating a night looking at the stars, not knowing it was the last night she would get to do anything.

The last few pages of the diary are blank.

Something raw and slippery tingles around my fingers. My sister had curated her death. She was supposed to be a drowned angel in the lake. For years to come, people would visit that bloody house and talk about the girl in the fur coat who walks around the lake, looking lost. Brownies on school trips would retell the ghost story over campfires. Emma would be a site of historical interest. But it didn't end up that way. It ended up very different to that.

Where does someone's energy go when their body is cracked open? Does it end up in the corners of all the bedrooms they visited, nestled in the hearts of everyone they knew? Do they have their own secret portals through which they come in and out of the world, where we can sometimes feel them? And if they're an artist, does their influence go even deeper, into places inside people that they didn't even know they had?

141

It made think of how my mum made an effort to ensure I didn't read any newspapers after Emma died. What had Mum wanted to hide? The agitation that the diary entry left in me provoked a need to walk. I made my way, a little dazed, along the beach and up through the village to the library near the village square. I had never looked for archived newspaper reports before. I kept thinking about when detectives looked through some sort of screen when they did it in films. The stoner with the earphones round his neck didn't bother to ask me for ID, and directed towards me towards a back corner, where folded newspapers in blue folders were pressed tightly against each other in a wall-to-wall stack.

For a few hours, I went through all of them, darting between the stack and a sticky circular table. Old women in Zimmer frames returned Mills and Boon paperbacks, and men in plaid trousers leafed through Colin Forbes novels. At one point I gave up, and almost decided no one had written anything about my sister and that she probably hadn't existed. I left the papers strewn about and went and bought sausage and chips and burnt my mouth eating them while I sat on the village bench. Then I got back to work.

I was cursing my own lack of academic ability and thinking how I needed to devise some sort of system when I stumbled across something that sent a cold shiver through my fingertips.

Overdose victim Emma Imrie knew she was in danger hanging out with Adam Wolf, inquest hears

Rising star of Camden scene Emma Imrie knew she was "putting herself in danger" with her entry into London's drug addled underworld, her mother told inquest.

Miss Imrie, recently signed to cult label Foxhole, was not a drug addict, and her London move was "purely for career reasons" said her mother.

By Ernest Allen
3:31PM GMT 07 February 2001

Despite feeling vulnerable, Imrie 'stuck it out' at a party in a run-down stately home with the inner circle of London's indie musicians. Her intention was to secure career success, according to her mother.

But hours later, the 19-year-old granddaughter of Ralph Imrie, the noted investment banker, died from heroin poisoning at the Hertfordshire home of James Tighe on 19th October.

The circumstances leading up to the musician's death emerged during an inquest at London's Coroner Court.

Her mother, Josephine Imrie, told how she had seen her daughter in a hospital in East London a week before her death, after she had taken what she believes was an accidental drug overdose. Her mother said she was suffering from nervous exhaustion and was distraught after having broken up with her boyfriend, Adam Wolf, of the cult band Rosary.

Rosary sprang to fame following a major record deal and a series of high-profile London performances from which members of the band drew criticism for glamourising self-harm. One outspoken critic of the group said, "Wolf has become the toxic Pied Piper of the Camden Crowd. Wherever he goes, a trail of lovesick bulimics follow, trying to outdo each other in the shock stakes to secure the attention of this sneering king of the court." Others have praised the bands intelligent, state-of-the-nation lyrics. His single 'Council Pop' was an NME Single Of The Week.

Wolf was previously criticized for declaring admiration when a contemporary of his, the vocalist for the rock group Akimbo, committed suicide. Wolf commented, "It was the best thing for him to do. The world doesn't need any more white male singers making a career out of the fact that they couldn't sleep with the last girl they fancied."

But Imrie's mother dismisses such context. "Having spent a few days getting her back on her feet, Emma said she had to go back into London to meet with people from the record industry," she said. "I begged her not to go but, in the end, I had to accept I couldn't control her."

Imrie ended up at the home inherited by Tighe, who

previously worked as a publicist with the popular androgynous rock group Ashtray Cult.

Death Of A Riot grrrl: Emma Imrie was 'sucked into the toxic world of Adam Wolf' 30 Jan 2001

Mrs Imrie said that she later found out her daughter had met with people in Camden and ended up joining them for the party.

"She was very upset about the breakup, but I think she thought that meeting would help her meet people on her path to getting a major record deal. She thought career success was the best way to move on from her breakup. Or perhaps at least show she was moving on."

"I understand that she went to the party at Tighe's house purely for career purposes," she added. "It was unfortunate that there were drugs there when she was in a fragile state."

Emma Imrie's band Cherub had begun to build a cult following due to their intense and energetic live performances. The band was establishing itself as a feature of the emerging feminist Riot grrrl scene, a scene that originated in the U.S. Their song 'Hairy Food' drew particular attention for a protagonist that vocalised the worldview of an anorexic. The band drew comparisons to artists such as Bikini Kill and Babes In Toyland.

On the subject of her daughter's mental state, Mrs Imrie said, "Emma had confided in me that she had not taken drugs in the past, and the reason for her initial overdose had been because she was in a state following the breakup. But she was clear to me she had no intention of taking drugs again and I really don't think that's why she went back to London.

"She was well aware that, in the music scene, she was working in a kind of dangerous situation and she went into that with her eyes open but despite that she got caught up in something."

Mrs Imrie last spoke to her daughter by phone on the night before she died, and she told her that she had to stay another night in order to hang out at an informal gathering, which she'd feared was a party.

"She mentioned the party would be in a stately home and that people there would be dodgy, but she kept saying, "I am being strong," and, "I won't be tempted again," Mrs Imrie said.

Just hours before her death, footage showed her smoking crack cocaine out of a brandy bottle improvised into a pipe while sat next to Vince Ellis, the frontman of the band Ashtray Cult.

The following morning, a partygoer found her in a room in a remote part of the house. A Miriam Simms went to wake her, discovered her unresponsive body, and promptly called the police.

Professor Gilbert Hurst, consultant toxicologist at Kings College hospital, told the court that she had died from heroin poisoning, although levels in her blood were not high, she was a 'naïve' user.

A post-mortem showed that she had cocaine traces in her system, but these are not thought to have contributed to her death.

Professor Hurst said, "I think it is noteworthy that there was not a history of regular heroin use because, in my opinion, the cause of death was heroin poisoning.

"Heroin is an extremely toxic drug, especially in someone that hasn't been taking it regularly before. People need to appreciate that you can't play with it.

"Even though the concentration of heroin in the blood was relatively low, it doesn't mean that the effect of morphine causing respiratory depression could not have caused death."

PC Colin Antony added, "A search of the house found there were crack pipes, and in the bathroom, there was a purse full of syringes.

"There was dried blood spattered on the walls, which was used to write some disturbing messages. It is not the kind of place I would expect a woman from such a family to end up in, let alone to die. It had a bit of a cult feel to it, a sense that was exacerbated by the house's remote location."

After officers investigating the tragedy viewed the filmed

footage, Tighe was jailed for six months for possession of crack, and another partygoer, Luke Turner, was jailed for twelve months for supplying the Class A drug. He was also given a three-year conditional discharge for possession.

A blazing row with Adam Wolf led to the breakup which began the downward spiral, according to Mrs Imrie.

"They had an argument about him being unsupportive regarding her career," she said. "She felt he was being uncaring towards her, and he in turn accused her of being too needy."

Wolf said of the accusation, "I don't think Emma would have done anything self-destructive on purpose. I think it is a tragic thing that happened, but it's because of bad luck."

When pushed on whether he had treated her poorly in the way he broke up with her, Wolf replied, "I was aware she was upset that I had been spending time with people she didn't like, but the nature of my work is that I have to live quite a free-spirited lifestyle. In the end there was an incompatibility there, but I didn't contribute in any way to what happened."

When asked if he was to blame for introducing her to the drugs scene Wolf replied, "You would have to blame London if you went down that way of thinking, and Emma chose to move there."

Mrs Imrie said, "I do feel that with a bit more kindness, Adam could have shielded my daughter from the darker elements of London. I know it is all part of the rock 'n roll dream, but for all that, my daughter could seem worldly. She was, in fact, very young, insecure and scared. When someone is charismatic, as she was, people can forget that underneath is just a very frightened young girl.

"She told me Adam had dumped her over the phone and was very upset. When we stayed with her in hospital, she kept saying he had made her feel worthless. I think she was embarrassed at having made such a show of moving to London to succeed as a singer and wanted to demonstrate that a heartless breakup would not stop her."

DS Jon Killingsworth, who investigated the death, said that Emma was seen on her film taking drugs and he had been told by partygoers that she had mentioned being upset Wolf was not at the party. He said that the footage gave him the impression she was taking the heroin 'in a conspicuous way in order to worry him'.

He added, "It shows Emma holding a piece of tin foil over a tin foil tube which is consistent with her smoking heroin. That suggests to me someone had shown her how to do this if she was inexperienced." When pushed to say whether she might have been doing this to draw attention to herself, Killingsworth replied, "I wouldn't like to say. She was either trying to ingest a serious dose or she wanted people to think that she was."

A crack pipe, sharps bin and more than thirty pieces of tin foil were found in the blood-spattered room alongside her body.

Simms, who discovered the body of Imrie, said, "I realised she had not moved out of the room for a while, and alarm bells rang when I went and tried to wake her, and she was cold. I knew in my heart that something had gone badly wrong and I regretted not checking earlier. But she didn't know anyone at the party, so no one had been keeping an eye on her. I stroked her on the forehead, and she felt cold."

When asked what her impression was of Miss Imrie. Simms said, "That she was a vibrant, warm, intelligent, open and highly talented young woman. My impression was she was only a part of this scene to try and win the approval and attention of Mr Wolf. She was not the only one there who had that motivation either."

Adam Wolf has previously drawn criticism for his relationship with his fans. An anonymous source linked to Mr Tighe said, "There is a cult of personality around Adam and, in some cases, to get his approval people have mimicked his self-destructive ways. At some of the parties held at [Tighe's] there had been sadomasochistic sexual practices as well as heroin use, and Wolf was very much the ringleader. There was almost a sense that the more risqué you were, the more he would approve, and I fear Emma was caught up in that mindset. The fact that these practices had moved out of drug dens in London and into more grand setting proves there was a sense of momentum about the behaviours as well as possibly backing from wealthy parties."

The verdict by Dr Hayes was that Miss Imrie died of misadventure.

He said, "The unintended consequence of her taking a relatively small amount or infrequently using heroin over the last week of her life was that she received a level of morphine in her blood that was toxic to her. It led to her respiratory depression that caused her death in her sleep."

I pulled the pages out, folded them and pushed them into my pocket. Everyone in the village would have read it but me, and that thought angered me. No wonder I felt like the ghost at the banquet.

At least by fitting it all together with her diary entries I felt like I understood why she did what she did. Not because of record company contracts, perhaps in part because she wanted Adam to know what he had done to her, that he had sent her to the edge. But most of all she had done it to try and block the world out, a world that, in every one of her diary entries, she had found brutal, cold, unsympathetic.

I knew exactly how she felt. Had she wanted to leave that world, or merely get very close to leaving it? Perhaps it was all in an attempt to see it for what it really was, so she could better live with it.

I suspected the latter. I suspected it because I now knew what it was like to have that feeling.

Chapter Twenty-Three

In the days that followed I made solitude an art form. I didn't really think about Mum and Dad, and what they might think about my situation. I'd go to River's for a few hours in the evening. It was good to know that, at least, his house existed, like a distant sandbank for a weary swimmer, somewhere in the expanse of leaves beyond Bembridge fort. I knew that I would be alone all day but that at least I could be with people in the evening if I needed to. It's amazing how much solitude you can take, as long as it feels like an option. I was glad to be alone as well. It meant that at least no one else was screwing me up.

Once, when I was leaving River's house, Ruth called me from the doorway. I turned and noticed she had this weird expression on her face. She said, "You're not really sleeping on the beach, are you?"

"I'm fine," I said.

"Because you can still have the annexe," she added.

"Thanks," I replied, before turning away.

"Jeff, I didn't scare you out of the annexe, did I?" she asked, sweeping the hair from her face.

"No, not at all," I answered, turning back.

"Because you don't have to put up with me getting into bed with you if you don't want me to," she said, with a hint of a smile.

"It's not that," I said. "I liked you doing that."

"Yeah." Her eyes traced around mine after she spoke. "You *loved* it, didn't you?"

I smiled for the first time in days. "Oh, shut up," I said.

She skipped away, laughing.

Most mornings I awoke to a blistering sun. It beat through the canvas of the tent. The sea felt so close I was sure it'd be painful to leave it when the summer ended. I swam, I cut my feet on pebbles, and I found ways to rub off the sand as I dried myself under the shade of the trees. I'd then tramp up to the Happy Shopper.

One day I went to the newsagent and, having browsed the dusty, out-of-date goods, I rifled through the cassettes in his bargain bin. I imagined that a Cherub cassette was in there somewhere, like a treasure buried in the sand - Emma rediscovered. I'd had so many dreams about being in record stores and finding all these deluxe versions of albums by her that I never knew she made. Even though there was no tape, the feeling of wanting to find it became so potent I thought I'd seen it sometimes. But one morning I came across Adam's debut album, this slender cassette box. It had stylish embossed gold artwork with black lettering. Looking over my shoulder at the newsagent, I took it out of its sleeve and unravelled the inlay card. There was a shot of each band member, one in the bath showing his veins, another glowering in the corner of a bedroom. In the one of Adam, he was wearing a black striped suit jacket and Emma's chiffon scarf, and he had one arm folded over the other with his eyes closed.

It made me shudder.

On what felt like her bidding, I stole notebooks and biros. Emma had taught me how to steal.

Under the trees on the beach I scribbled my fantasies for a future life. I imagined myself as the signer in a Camden band, jamming in sweat-lined cellars, eating dodgy wraps on balconies that overlooked the market then, in the evening, playing at rammed club nights to crowds that adored me.

It was only when a bird cried overhead that I was shook from my reverie and back into a world of dried mud and sea. I tucked the notebook into my sock and wondered how filthy I must have looked. Emma's blue silk shirt had mud on it. I stared at the sea and decided that my state of mind was a secret

I had to closely guard.

I knew I was eating less and that the situation with the ulcers in my mouth was getting out of hand. That day I couldn't face another moment of looking at the sea, as if it had answers. So, in the evening sun, I began the walk up to the lifeboat station, just to see if I could at least spy River's house from there. I was in such a state of loneliness that just the thought of watching real people felt like a comfort.

I hadn't bargained on the fact that it was a unique night. Once a year, the tide was so low that people were able to walk from the beach, around the Napoleonic forts a good mile out to sea. As I walked, I could see ahead of me in the fading light the orange glow of various bonfires, as people held summer barbeques on the beach for the expedition parties. I could see the walkers, in distant winding snakes, treading their way through the sand and the clay, to the small black cap of a fort nestling on the horizon.

They seemed a perfect metaphor for the way I saw people; distant, all consumed with a joint task that seemed utterly pointless to me. On the sand, mums and girlfriends and labradors of various hues waited for their return with well-tended fires and thick towels.

Stepping around these parties just made me feel worse. I was like the ghost at the banquet, the unkempt guy stepping through their social bubbles. What place did I have in their fantasy lives? People toasted sesame seed buns on sticks and ate salads off their knees. They drank beers and sang along to beloved songs on portable stereos. Their sunglasses were tipped up to a blue summer sky and smiles were etched on their faces. And the girls, the girls at these parties made me feel as if *my* heart had been skewered and then barbequed. There were girls dressed in white cardigans, or with boyfriend's sweaters over their shoulders. With all their laughter and their perfume and their air of femininity I felt like they were a chorus of angels, laughing at me from up in heaven. I was sure there was no one out there that felt as alone as I did. That made it all the more strange when I looked out and saw, in the distance, a swathe of blue water and standing

151

in it a young woman in a black bikini throwing a mane of thick, sea-drenched black hair over her head. The droplets flew from the tips of it and studded the sky for a moment, catching the evening sun. I waited for her inevitable boyfriend to emerge from the water, but she was definitely alone. As I walked, I tried not to stare at her. But there was something about her hard posture. She seemed embedded in the sand and that transfixed me. There was something powerful about the loop of muscles in her torso, the clenched thighs, ripples emanating from them. She looked so uncompromising, a fixture in the frozen water that wasn't prepared to negotiate with it. I thought for a moment that this woman had somehow tamed the sea, and I envied her.

I kept walking. At every party along the beach the sense of camaraderie oozed from the people, but the sense of warmth just seemed to taunt me. The way people pulled dogs out of my way or lifted the corners of rugs, so I didn't tread on them, all served to make my heart feel even heavier. I was being treated like a pariah, an embarrassment. I trudged my sense of anger and hurt into the sand and just kept moving.

For all my momentum, I had no sense of purpose. Somehow my brain found one. There was a long square fence bordering the field above the sea. There was probably a mile of squared fence. I just decided that I was going to walk on top of the whole thing however long it would take me.

I started at the tree stooped over the ocean and used its branches to get me onto the fence. I walked along the fence, pausing sometimes to regain my balance when I wobbled. I must've stood there at one point for twenty minutes, waiting until I got my balance before I took the next step. Life, I decided, was all about mental discipline. I was convinced that this rigour would benefit me in years to come. I was learning not to take the next step until I was completely balanced. As I walked, a step at a time, I thought how lucky I was to have the time to strengthen weak parts of my brain, how other people probably never had these developed places in their minds that they could return to at any time in the future, if needed.

I was about three quarters round the fence when it

happened. I slipped, and a rusty nail dragged its way up my calf. It split, like a plump chicken breast opening for a sharp knife. There was this pretty big gush of blood.

It stung and, in a moment, my heart started pulsing harder than it ever had done. I limped over to the tap where people washed their feet as they came off the beach. I tried to staunch the wound with my hands and with the water, but the bleeding wouldn't stop. My heart was racing faster. I'd never seen so much blood and although part of me badly wanted help I couldn't face the thought of someone screaming if they saw the situation. I was determined to fix it by myself.

But I couldn't. No matter how much I tried to push the wound shut it gaped open and yawned blood, and the water diluted it, but didn't stop it. The more I tried to use my fingers to seal it, the more I realised how dirty my fingers were, and that made me panic too. There was no one around this evening, they were all on the beach. I realised I was too far from anywhere to get help. So I started crying. I realised I was so hungry, and so tired, and so angry, and in so much pain, and whatever I did or thought nothing changed the facts and that damn blood just wouldn't stop coming out.

I sat down and decided to just push the wound shut until it stopped. But it didn't and blood kept leaking everywhere.

Then I passed out.

Chapter Twenty-Four

It was a splash of water on my face that woke me. I felt something on my eyebrows. Was it dried blood? As I looked up, I saw Ruth's face, all thick lips and worried eyes. "Drink this," she ordered.

The heat had left the air, but the place still felt empty. As I looked down, I saw that she'd ripped a sleeve off her denim shirt and used it to stop the bleeding. The bind sat there on my calf, this big, ridiculous knot. Blood-soaked denim. There was loads more blood than I remembered, all dried on the dusty concrete.

"We need to get that properly cleaned," she said. Her hair was wet, and I realised she was the woman I'd watched swimming. What was it about the situation I'd seen her in that had stopped me recognising her? "Get up. For God's sake, Jeff," she said. "Enough is enough."

"I'm fine," I said. "I just need to get back to my stuff."

"You're not fine," she said. "You're coming back with me. This ends now."

She helped me to my feet. I knew it was a long walk back to her house, with my arm around her shoulder.

"Put your arm around me," she ordered.

I did as I was told. Again. "How did you know I was here?" I asked.

"I didn't," she said. "But because I'm not utterly heartless, I've been taking evening walks in this direction. Just to keep a vague eye on you."

She didn't even try to hide it. She didn't care what I thought any more.

My leg seriously hurt when I walked. I could feel the blood squelch under the bind. "I suppose It's a good job you did," I said, and started limping.

"Yeah, no kidding," she replied.

I looked up the winding road, cool in the blue dark. "There's no way we're walking all the way to yours," I said.

She kept her eyes fixed on the leg. "What choice do we have? I don't have a car and there's no taxis round here. Everyone's at The Fort Walk. There's a phone to call 999, but the handset has been ripped off."

River, I thought.

"We'll just have to get there very slowly," she said. "I'll help you."

It was a long walk home. But it was also kind of good to have someone so close to me, for such a long period of time. Even if I knew I was being a pain with the limp. We walked in silence, just struggling up the long path to her house.

I couldn't remember the last time I'd spent so much time in someone's company. Just listening to them breathe. Smelling their scent. Feeling how strong and persistent they were. I had to admit, I did need people. However hard I'd tried to completely get away from them I knew I would've been in real trouble if I'd have succeeded tonight. I looked at Ruth, the lock of hair that fell over her face as she looked down at my leg. The way it curled and caught the sun.

"What do we do now?" I said, when we got to her gate.

"We sort you out," she said.

That night I had a bath with my big denim knot, and a shave and afterwards in the living room Ruth cleaned the wound with some ointment she had found. Every dab stung, and I was glad River was staying in Seaview so he couldn't make fun of me. Ruth kept saying, "Sorry, sorry," as she dabbed it. It felt kind of good to have her hands on my leg, to every now and then have her look up at me with this little smile. She spent a long time cleaning the wound, even when it looked pretty sorted to me.

I had to admit, she'd patched my leg up pretty good. And I liked the look of concentration on her face as she kept saying, "Sorry, sorry, sorry!" with a smile as she kept ripping off and moving the plaster until she thought she'd got it right. "We'll

155

get you in at the GP tomorrow," she said. "I'll fetch your stuff off the beach if you tell me where it is. I'm not hearing any excuses about it either. You could've died."

"I guess I'll be sleeping in the annexe then," I said, checking out all the plasters on my legs.

"Not tonight," she said, standing up. "You're sleeping in my bed."

"What?"

"So I can keep an eye on you."

She got up and went into the kitchen. I looked out at the darkened garden, where River and I had played football so many times. What would he make of this?

When she returned, Ruth had put some hot casserole and bread and butter on a tray. As I ate, she fetched and then poured me some red wine. "To take the edge off," she said. Next to it was a couple of painkillers.

I felt pretty ravenous. She tried not to widen her eyes as I finished off the tray. Without saying anything she went and refilled the plate, and watched TV while I devoured seconds, and thirds. It was like there was a hole in me.

"I'm going to watch some crap on TV," she said. "Get some sleep in my bed."

It might've only been a few hours later when she pulled up the covers. I hadn't drawn the curtains and had collapsed the moment I'd lay down. The sky in the window over her head was a kind of dark blue, and I felt from her bare legs that Ruth was wearing an oversized white shirt as she got in. She pressed her body against me, her breasts warm, her thighs smooth and her feet cold. I felt her fingers sleek gently through my hair. I closed my eyes. She was whispering something. Her other hand reached over my chest and took mine. I clasped it tight, and as she rubbed her thumb over my knuckles, I found myself, in some wordless exchange of deeply felt emotion, rubbing my thumb back against her hand. I shut my eyes tight. I wanted the feel of her fingers in my hair, the warmth of her caresses to never stop. I had never expressed as much as I did through my thumb as I massaged her hand.

"How are you feeling?" she asked.

I let the pillow absorb my tears and then I sat up. "Thank you so much for helping me," I croaked.

She smoothed out the covers in front of her. "No problem. Listen Jeff, your parents really haven't been there for you. You know that, don't you?"

I nodded. "But you have."

"It's not like I don't care about you."

"It's not like I don't care about you, either," I said.

She tucked a lock of hair over her ear and kept looking at the covers. "Really?" she asked.

I put my arms around her. I could smell her recently washed hair, and the slight scent of red wine on her lips. "Really," I whispered.

She turned and looked up at me. The moment she opened her mouth I kissed her. She moaned and kissed me back, with such force that she pushed me back onto the pillow.

Her body felt strong, and tender. She pressed her chest hard against me, and as she straddled me, I realised she could feel me through my boxer shorts. She took my head in both of her hands. "Are you sure you want this?" she asked.

I nodded. There was this hunger in my body I hadn't known before. "Definitely," I said. The craving to feel close to someone had burst from its moorings.

She got up, smoothed her hair, and went out of the room. When she came back in, she had this condom in silver foil.

"Where did you get that?" I asked.

"River's room." She smiled, as she threw it to me. "It's not like he'll be using it any time soon. He has over a hundred."

I laughed and turned my back on her as I slipped it on. The moment I moved to her she kissed me, and she whimpered as our bodies clamoured closer and closer. She pulled back for a moment. "This feels right, doesn't it?" she asked.

I looked her in the eye. "Definitely," I said. I told myself not to say anything else.

"We'll just have to be gentle," she said.

She reached down and bit her lip as she closed her eyes. She eased me inside her, and I could not believe that wet, tight

157

sensation. I forgot all about the pain as she eased me inside her, and she kept kissing me. She pulled off her t-shirt, and her heavy breasts pressed against me. Her body felt familiar, and yet strangely powerful. She closed her eyes and pushed down onto me. And we kept kissing and kissing.

Chapter Twenty-Five

I lay in Ruth's bed the next morning and couldn't remember feeling so at ease. I didn't want to leave, and I wondered why I had ever chosen a mosquito-ridden bank by the sea to this.

Next to me, Ruth pored through my stories as if they were some sort of map. My small notebook must have fallen out of the pocket of my shorts. She had a notebook at her side, and she sighed, loud, as she made inscriptions I couldn't see. Sunlight blasted over the bed and the side of her face. I could see birds skittering through the sky at her far shoulder.

The Verve burbled quietly from the stereo at the foot of the bed, which her socked foot bounced on. I took in the Friends collage above her desk, by the door. A series of quotes and shots of funny moments from the series, that she seemed to have picked out and then glued on from a pack. Chandler was stuck in a fixed grimace, the girls laughing at him. I thought of how I had woken up yesterday on a beach as a virgin, and how today it was as if my new life had begun. On her neatly arranged desk I could see annotated copies of Henry James novels and collections of Shakespeare plays. The multi-coloured tabs suggested heavy annotations inside.

Sunlight was pouring through the window, lighting the whole room in a gold glow. I wondered if I had died by the beach and gone to heaven. But I wouldn't have imagined anywhere as nuanced as this and so knew that wasn't the case.

"Feel free to read something," she said, turning to me with a smile. I wondered if she'd worn such heavy eye-makeup before. The pink feather boa resting over one corner of her bed looked new. It hadn't been there last night. Just being amongst a girl's belongings felt nourishing. As I moved over to the stereo I took in the slanted pile of CDs by the speaker.

159

"Try not to make fun of them," she said, rolling onto her back.

The covers all seemed to be of moody shots of 1970s style houses and cafes. The bands were called Rialto, Ether, Grass Show. I was drawn in by a copy of Pulp's 'Common People', the band lined up against the window of a Formica-topped cafe. It seemed to me to summarise a world I craved.

"Have you seen the new poster?" she asked.

She pointed at the door. On the back of it was a poster with the words 'Pulp: Different Class'. Under the six frames of the band members within it was the motto 'Please Understand. We Just Want The Right To Be Different. That's all.' I leaned forward. In each picture the band members were shot in black and white, ghostly against the coloured backdrops of various English scenes, images of tacky days at the seaside, flirtations by the school fence, acrylic discos.

I felt enchanted and scared by the poster. It seemed to herald the new existence I was about to have, now that I was an adult.

The bouncing tom-toms of Oasis' 'Live Forever' came on the stereo. I looked back to see Ruth murmur something about my story. Knowing that at any moment she was going to tell me what she thought of my writing-that for the first time I would hear what *anyone* thought of it only added to the sense that I was on the precipice of something.

The situation seemed to exist out of time. I knew Ruth was about to offer me a verdict. And I knew that her presence in my life would nourish me and take me forward. I knew that the mad scribblings I had done on the beach were just the start of something. Like the froth that came out of the champagne bottle the moment you opened it, I knew that there would be something with more substance to come.

I had the feeling too that I'd return to these fleeting moments of that sunlit morning again and again, when a world of music and sex and writing and dancing was opening up to me, like a lotus, when I was scared of the world but also excited by it. I knew that those few seconds, when Ruth shut my book, sat on the edge of the bed and turned towards me, had a teetering sense of magic about them.

I could hardly stand the swinging sense of expectation. "What do you think?" I asked.

She smiled. "Are you kidding me?" she said. She tapped the page. "This writing is dark, scary. But good."

I hadn't heard this word used in relation to something I'd made.

"Thanks," I said, blushing.

"You obviously miss her a lot," she said, lolling her head back on a pillow. She started rummaging for something in the storage unit under her bed.

"Yeah," I said. I thought of the diary. "It's more that there's nothing left. It's more that she can't surprise me."

"I've got something that you might find interesting," she said.

She pulled out videotape and moved to the squat TV on her bedside table. She inserted it, and then fiddled with a remote. I moved around to look at the screen. We lay next to each other, on our fronts.

It began with a shot of the top of a London escalator. I recognised the brittle guitar riff; thin, serrated.

I knew that it was the video of Emma's debut single. Something in my chest opened. It felt like petals were bursting from a box.

I gulped as *my sister* loomed into the top of the escalator and then roared onto the screen. My first thought was that she personified everything I was feeling about her at that time. She had dark eyes and blood red lips. The sound coming out of her mouth was angry, but sensual. It looked like she was wearing a black feather coat. I thought of the presence I'd sensed in the house the morning of her overdose. I realised this would not be the inane romp I had pictured in my mind. On what level had Emma been aware she was embodying the dark forces that were closing in around her?

Before I could work out what was going on, the shot cut to her in a grimy back alley. Her hand was on one hip as she languished on the bonnet of a battered Volvo. Emma looked sideways. Her cropped hair was so slick it looked a little wet.

161

Her leather jacket was so undersized it was almost a wrap. In the next shot, as the music built to the chorus, she was in her leopard-print coat, prancing in front of vintage stalls in London. She was confronting, joking, and then she was frolicking on an Essex beach with dripping ice-cream cone.

Her band mates were whirling on a shining carousel behind her in a bizarre clash of outfits. They cavorted for the camera, back to back. They rubbed themselves, pouted, scowled. In the few moments that the shot lingered on each of them they auditioned to be stars in their own right: Donna, laughing with maternal confidence, Melissa, squirming with teenage sexuality, and Simone, a rabbit in the headlines, her spots just visible under the cheap foundation, her headdress slipping from the back of her head.

Emma's lyrics were about lipstick stains, walks of shame, closing time. She was a lioness announcing her arrival. She winked at us, and her expression said, 'Get used to me'. It was a promise made with more sharpness and passion than I had imagined, and relieved as I was to discover this new aspect of her, it frightened me too. But then the shot blinked shut, Emma sashaying into the distance. She'd gone, and she'd barely announced her arrival.

I wanted to protest. I wanted to tell them I hadn't been able to revel in the 'getting used to her' she'd promised in that wink. But there was no one I could complain to. There was just fuzz on the screen as the clip ended. In Emma's only pop video, she flails at various personas and decides on nothing. She is merely living, her loose ends flapping around, unresolved. She is just like all of us.

"I've watched this video so many times. Is that weird?" Ruth asked, as she pressed the stop button.

"No. What's weird is that I've never seen it before." I looked at her. I wanted to say something, but my mouth was too dry to form words. It was like in a dream when you want to shout, but can't make a sound. I forced myself to say the words, "Thank you for that."

"You thought you'd never get to see anything new about her, didn't you?"

"She's still surprising me then," I said, with a smile.

That's her at her peak, I thought. That's the moment the star streaked across the sky, the moment she got to play out all her fantasies and prove her potential, when all that elbow grease paid off, when all her eccentricities and bizarre lyrics were justified for the three minutes she was a star. And if it wasn't for Ruth, I might never have got to see that.

I looked at her and felt something I hadn't felt before.

I heard a pounding on the stairs. Ruth looked at me, and for a moment seemed to wonder if she should get up from the bed, or perhaps I should? River was shouting her name. Something else was about to change as well. She exchanged an expression with me that looked to me for guidance. But my expression was blank enough to be totally unhelpful. The door opened. River took a glance at Ruth and me sat on the edge of her bed like nuns.

"Well this is the least surprising plot twist ever," he said. "Do you two actually have sex then, or do you just weep in each other's arms until hydration sets in?"

Ruth looked at me and then at River. "Come on then. Keep it coming," she said.

He folded his arms and leaned against the doorway. "I take it you're now going to become some lame literary type, then Jeff. With leather elbow patches and..." He seemed to flail around for words. "A spiral bound notebook," he finished, eventually.

Ruth stood up. "You lost your way with that notebook bit, didn't you?" she asked.

"You'd better still be coming to the Wheeler's party tonight," he said to me.

"Why?"

"Because I promised them you'd come."

"What he means is, you're his entry ticket because you're the one with the famous sister," Ruth jibed.

River shot her a glance. "Whereas my sister will only ever have a reputation for getting off with her younger brother's mates," he replied.

She turned to me. "I haven't got off with any of his other

mates," she said, doing air quotes.

"Don't worry. I'm still joining you tonight, River," I said.

"Good," River said, turning towards the door. "Because some *proper* girls were asking if you were coming tonight, and I assured them you were," he said.

"I'm pretty sure that I count as a *proper* girl," Ruth said, using air quotes. "I mean, I have the used tampons to prove it, if you like."

"Yeah. Please don't," River said, turning to leave the room.

Ruth looked at me and bit her lip. "Well we wouldn't want to disappoint any proper girls now, would we?"

"Are you sure you don't fancy coming?"

She put her hands on my shoulders. "No. It's time for you to join the land of the living. You're a big boy now." She patted me on the bum, with what I assumed was a sense of irony.

"This is beyond gross," River said. "Come on, Jeff, let's have some hustle. The buses go about once every three days and I need to check out the talent at the Cadet Week disco before the party."

'Talent' seemed a curious way of describing a bunch of adolescents enjoying their first experience of a disco. But under the circumstances I decided to let it go.

Chapter Twenty-Six

I felt a sense of melancholy as we approached the sailing club. As we walked up to the wooden doors of the clubhouse, nestled above the sea, I remembered all those feelings I'd had at my first disco. It had been in the town hall, when the lilting reggae of Chaka Demus & Pliers and the plinky keyboards of Whigfield's 'Saturday Night' had filled me with a kind of wanderlust, when River and I had taken it in turns to try and screw up the courage to ask girls to dance, before going off and then reconvening to lie to each other about the number of dance partners we'd now had, when my real number had remained fixed at a static zero. The one time I had asked a girl she'd said, "There's no way in hell I'm dancing with you, Jeff."

River was swigging from a bottle of white wine, stolen, I presumed, from his parents' drinks cabinet. "They'll throw us out if we drink in there," he said. "Before I unleash myself on the ladies, some Dutch Courage."

He stood at the top of the stone steps that disappeared under the boat rack. I followed his gaze down the murky stairwell where the sea-battered steps appeared to reduce into wet shingle.

"Fancy a couple of leaps?" he asked.

"Go on then."

During our younger days, jumping off things was our favourite pastime. River stepped back into the road, forcing a Ford Cortina to do an emergency stop. He took a run up and then leapt off the top step and down into the darkness. I hadn't had time to wonder if jumping down a flight of stone steps onto even more stones was such a bright idea. I looked into the gloom as he let out a yelp.

"You alright?"

I couldn't see him.

"Bottom step," he finally announced. "Beat that."

The disco music was thudding, loud. A woman was singing "Do you think you're better off alone?" The lights, in circles of primary colours, were spinning on the inside of the tarpaulin. I was either in there or out here, I thought.

"Get out the way then," I said.

Chapter Twenty-Seven

The disco under the tarpaulin was heaving. In various corners of the attached bar, teenagers sipped Coca Colas and spied on each other with wide eyes. The girls danced in small, self-conscious groups, the bright sparkle of their sequins suggesting dresses worn for the first time. River abandoned me the moment we entered. I found him in the bar, after a few circles of the disco, during which I'd tried to feign a general air of apathy. I could see the girl who'd rejected my only offer to dance, her dark hair had since been cut into a sophisticated bob. She had become even prettier and was wearing a sweater with a heart on it. There was something about her gamine features that suggested a society beauty in the making, and the thought of that made me feel sick. I'd been rejected by someone because I wasn't good enough for them, and there was no getting away from it.

A row of young girls were holding their drinks and watching River by the bar. They had fallen into two natural columns, and River was taking his shoes off at the end of it. He tested the floor with his toes. "Not ideal, as work surfaces go," he said. "Carpet's probably my best medium. Lino can go either way."

"You can't do a flip in here!" shouted a ginger boy that I knew to be called Mostyn. He leant in to a girl next to him. "He couldn't do one anywhere," he added, with confidence.

River rubbed his hands. "If the room was bigger, I could probably fit in two." He nudged a girl in a red dress. "I bet you've heard that before, haven't you?" he asked. There were some confused ripples of laughter. River arched back, stretching his spine.

"It's not easy, being a regionally acclaimed gymnast," he

167

announced. "I'm coveted. Handpicked." He stretched his arms. "An increasingly commercial proposition."

"You're a twat," shouted Mostyn.

"You're going to hurt yourself," said a girl. I followed the voice. It was her.

River looked at her and winked. "I'm dedicating this flip to all the girls everywhere, but especially to you," he said.

She giggled.

He took a small breath and ran the gauntlet. He threw himself onto his hands, kicked his legs over and landed on his feet. The crowd gasped in shock and awe. As he got to his feet, the braid in his hair stuck to the corner of his mouth. He looked dazed, and he staggered into a table as he recovered himself.

"Fluke," shouted Mostyn. "Charlatan. Snake oil salesman."

The girl had a small smile on her face as she watched to see what River would do next. "Is he alright?" she asked a friend. I decided that the risk of hurting myself might be the only way to get the attention of a girl like her. I started to wonder if it would be worth asking River to teach me to do flips. But the thought of him indulging in how hard it was to teach someone without his raw talent dimmed my enthusiasm.

"If it was a fluke, could I do this?" River announced.

He craned back and, to appreciative 'oohs', fell onto his hands. He walked on them for a good three or four steps, just long enough to knock over a tray of sausage rolls and two bottles of Panda Pops. A girl screamed as some of the froth caught her white puffy dress. As if acknowledging there would inevitably be casualties when he got going, River flipped back onto his feet. Buoyed by the applause, he jumped onto a table and took an extravagant bow. The room clapped. River, for one moment, looked relaxed.

"Right. You. Out."

I followed the sound of the bark. A balding man in a waistcoat was lifting the flap of his bar. "This is the last thing I need," he said. He had a look of intent about him, the air of someone who had no problem carrying two full bin bags at once.

"Time to go to the party," River said, pointing our way to the exit. He grabbed me by the elbow. "My famous friend and I are going to a massive party," he announced. "Later, sailboat wankers."

The girl turned to her friend. "What party do you think they are going to?" she asked.

Chapter Twenty-Eight

River and I had approached the white, slightly squat mansion overlooking the bay with very different feelings. He had listed the girls he thought would be going, along with their physical attributes. I had been thinking about Ruth, and last night, and thinking how I'd much rather have hung out with her. Besides, I had a pretty strong feeling that 'the girls' would be pretty indifferent to my arrival, and that River had sold me on a ticket that he didn't need to sell. As we rang the bell and hoped that the people partying above us would hear, I had the distinct feeling I was being pulled between two worlds.

We were welcomed by a ginger boy in a Super Mario t-shirt. "John, this is Jeff, as discussed," River said, as if confirming the dullest part of an exchange. "Come in then," John said, scanning behind us and then wincing when he clearly didn't find what he wanted.

River and I made our way through the roomy house, taking in huge paintings of African landscapes, walking over Tunisian rugs and up the stairs to the balcony that overlooked the bay. The Red Hot Chilli Peppers were playing on a CD in the corner, and the terrace was full. I had never seen people dressed down in a way that was so dressed-up. Distressed deck shoes and faded Fruit of the Loom jumpers suggested a determination to prove the guests were just beach bums.

John let us stand watching him as he gassed with a sandy blonde. Something in his manner gave off the impression that she was charming him in a manner that he was surprised by. It was as if he wanted us all to see the connection he was making with her in the moment. After a full five seconds of waiting River shouted, in his best Al Pacino voice, "Where's the booze? Flowing like mud around here." Everyone looked at him as he made his way over to a drinks cabinet in the corner. I walked to the edge of the balcony and took in the view.

I watched John pour Pimm's for the women. I accepted an opened bottle of Budweiser from River. It occurred to me that this was a party for people who'd been told they were special. It seemed a bit ironic I was here because of Emma, when Emma would've hated these people. It was even more ironic that I had been used as bait when I was possibly the only person here who'd never been told they were special. Except, perhaps, by Ruth.

I leaned against the railing, having decided to establish my attitude somewhere between friendly and wary. River crowded at my side. "The women here are all frigid." He craned to look over the side. "I wonder if I could jump to the ground."

A few hours later the sun began to set and the facades began to slip. I stayed next to the railing, as if chained to it. Ironically there'd been little apparent interest in me, except the occasional pointed finger and the snatched sound of my sister's name. I watched as a stain of scarlet bled into the china white of the sky. It was as if blotting paper had been caught, and I felt compelled to absorb the beauty of each moment. It was a need I hadn't experienced before. I savoured it. The crisp sea rolled in thin, long barrels to the shore. The crescent of gold sand curved into the horizon. I thought how even after all the things that had unhinged me, everything could still be all right. Had the dark cloud over me now passed?

But as people's drinks took hold, so a sense of occasion took grip. John pulled out an acoustic guitar and sat on a wicker chair in the centre of it all. An instructed nod to some lackey ensured the music was cut. The ringing notes from his guitar echoed out, the guitar figure a clumsy accompaniment to the sunset. River sat down and a pretty, snub-nosed girl lay her head on his shoulder. John, as if finally conceding that the time had come, raised the guitar up to me.

"Yes," said the girl on River's shoulder. "Give us a song, Jeff."

She'd never spoken to me before or, as far as I knew, looked at me. Everyone on the balcony turned to me. I realised

171

I didn't know how to play any sing-alongs. I knew my own songs, full of halting ideas. I knew my own lyrics, with their own clammy sentiments.

"Come on, then," John said, putting his feet up on the arm of his chair.

I took the guitar and sat in the chair next to John. It was as if this moment had been part of the program, and I'd been the only one not to know that. In a tense semi-circle, the whole of the balcony was watching me. I tried to form a chord with my hand but had suddenly forgotten them.

"Do Uptown Girl!" one woman shouted.

To my horror, the crowd took up the suggestion and roared their approval. "Yes!" they screamed. "Do Uptown Girl!"

"I-I don't know it," I stammered.

"Uptown Girl! Uptown Girl!"

I wasn't sure where the chant had started from, but after a heartbeat I felt as if I had been hearing it forever and that the mocking chant would never end.

"I promise. I don't know it," I stammered.

"What about some Nirvana?" someone shouted.

The idea of performing songs that had comforted me during bleak times to people who seemed to have never had any, made me feel ill.

"For Christ's sake, Jeff," River said. "Just play something. *Anything*."

I thought of Emma. What would she have done?

I thought of her diary entries, of what she had revealed. She'd have been glad people were paying her attention. She'd have made something of the moment.

I looked around. Everyone was folding their arms at me. A couple of the women moaned. "He's not going to play!" one said to her boyfriend.

I gripped the guitar and willed a solution to arrive.

"Play Time Of Your Life, Jeff," River suggested.

"Yes!" the crowd cheered.

"Do it. Now, Jeff," River said, through clenched teeth.

As I started to pluck the guitar, the folded arms around me unwound like a long rope. I began singing.

172

Some of the women made an 'aw' sound, and the men put their arms around the shoulders of their girlfriends. River sang along loudly, pulling the girl next to him into his cheek. I could feel eyes dissecting me, considering me.

When it got to the part where I sang the final line, I sang it with all the venom and sarcasm I could.

When the song ended, the crowd roared.

I felt so relieved that I thought I might shatter. I'd done it.

They were demanding another one.

River's expression suggested he knew not to ride his luck.

"John's turn!" he said, taking the guitar off me.

"Oh, go on then," John said, taking it.

River shook his head at me, as the attention was sloughed off onto our host. I exhaled. I felt as if I had run a gauntlet and survived. As if I had become a tiny bit stronger.

River was looking less enamoured. "Two words. Thin ice," he whispered.

His words smarted. "Two words. Up yours," I replied.

"Two more words. My sister," he said, patting me on the back. "Time to find a replacement," he added, taking a sip of beer.

Chapter Twenty-Nine

That night the party continued until well after all every bottle had been drained. At the point when River started conducting a mass sing-along of Bohemian Rhapsody on the balcony, I slipped outside. Under the darkening porch, lit only by nightlights, I could see a packet of cigarettes and a lighter waiting for some allotted time. I pulled a cigarette out and sparked it up.

"Jeff?"

I turned to see a girl's face, half-lit from inside the house. I recognised her from the disco earlier, the pretty Thai girl that had refused my awkward offer for a dance (as if we had been at some kind of 1950s high school prom) years ago. The applause of the crowd had buoyed me though, and for a few moments I felt as though that rejection had happened to someone else, that it couldn't have happened to me.

"Fancy a cigarette?" I asked.

"Can I share yours?"

"Let's sit on the sea wall. That way, if River falls in, I can enjoy the whole thing."

She laughed. We moved outside and sat down. She sat on her hands, her bare legs swinging from under her faint red shorts.

"I didn't know you could sing," she said.

"It's Melinda, isn't it?" I asked, with my new-found confidence. She nodded. "Neither did I. But it's a good job I could." I waved my cigarette up at the veranda. "Otherwise they'd have probably ripped me limb from limb."

She took the cigarette off me but didn't seem to know what to do with it.

"So I take it you're not having the best time."

"It's a blast," I said, watching her inhale with care.

"Not your kind of people?" she asked.

River had jumped onto the railing above us. He started to bawl We Are The Champions, but someone pulled him down. He fell, with a theatrical, 'Hey'.

"And who is your kind of person?" she asked, curling a lock of hair over her ear. "The famous River?"

I was reluctant to let on what a painful question I found it.

"River's River," I said, blowing smoke.

A strain of his singing reached us, and she giggled. "Oh yes. He's a rare talent," she said, looking out at the horizon. "An increasingly commercial proposition."

I laughed. "I don't know. He makes things happen. Don't you sometimes just want someone around who does that?"

"Yes. Yes, I think we all do," she said, thoughtfully.

She put her head on my shoulder. I watched the stub in my fingers and braced myself for its burn. Did I dare steal another? "I'm cold," she said.

I placed my arm around her. "Does that help?"

"A bit. But can we go inside?"

Chapter Thirty

When I woke up, I realised that she and I had slept, after a long and murmuring chat, on separate couches in the front room. My mind was full of couch corners, and the hot dreams of summer oceans that had distinguished my slumber. Melinda had left me alone at some point, and I wondered when.

The smell of bacon and the scent of flipped pancakes from the kitchen soon roused me. John was serving breakfast with the help of a few of the women from last night. Their faces were now scrubbed of makeup, their tresses held up by scarves.

I helped carry coffee back onto the balcony, which had been cleared of the night's debris. The revellers chomped pancakes using forks, and scraped rashers across plates from behind Wayfarer sunglasses. I ate ravenously, pouring syrup onto the pancakes and drinking coffee until I felt fully awake.

"I'm taking my hangover for a drink!" River said, announcing himself on the balcony with a lavish-looking cocktail. "And then I'm taking my drink for a swim."

A few of the women laughed. "You were in fine voice last night, River," John said, from behind his mirrored Aviators. There was a slight scent of skin oozing alcohol. The fragrance of brine from the sea, when it came with a cool gust of wind, was welcome.

Melinda arrived on the balcony, wearing the sweater with the heart on it. She looked composed as she sat next to me. "Did you get any sleep?" I asked.

"I want to go for a swim," she answered.

Standing on the sea wall with my hands on my hips, I worried for the first time how my body looked. The tattered blue boxer shorts I had on were unlikely to feature in an

Athena poster any time soon. When Melinda stepped outside, she looked naked except for a large white t-shirt, and she smiled at me as she squinted up at the sun.

A moment later, River pushed her past me and as he did, the gust delivered Melinda's girlish fragrance. River dived into the surf with a shout. She and I picked our way down the pebbles to the ocean. The morning ocean was transparent and lapped the sand with what seemed like caution. As River chopped out towards the horizon, she and I pushed our way through the shallows, ripples spreading like chevrons as we approached the web of sun lighting the surface.

When I next saw River, he was twenty feet out to sea, appearing like a seal-head between the illuminated varnishes of two moored bows. I felt relieved that his energy had taken him far away from the invisible bubble forming between Melinda and me.

She eased forward into the surf, which wetted the tips of her hair. "Wow," she said. "It feels nice. Are you not getting in?"

I crouched in the sea, a foot from her. The sunlight was raking over her wet hair. "Come on," she said, and in one incredible moment she opened her legs and wrapped them round me, pulling us both under the water. I got a quick sense of her slick body and then everything became bubbles and salt. When I broke to the surface, I was shocked to see her torso, her sodden t-shirt a second skin. I could see the shape of brown nipples under her t-shirt fabric and, for a second, I wondered if she was going to merge with me again. The sexual shock of the moment had been doused by the shocking cold of the water. She grasped one of my wet fingers and, with a reluctant smile, wrapped her wet legs around my back.

"Stop flirting and swim!" River shouted, from a long way away. His arms were flailing above the surface.

"I'm not going out that far," Melinda whispered. Her clean face, shining from sea, looked different. I trod water. I had only ever been close to Ruth's body before, and the memory of that clammy intimacy made me feel guilty. I had spent years craving girls and now all this was happening, when I'd done nothing to deserve it. The lines of drying seawater on

Melinda's freckled countenance, and her lopsided smile felt hard to resist.

I looked at the thick lock of hair plastered over her left ear, the lithe, wet body, which twisted to emphasise her breasts. I felt a surge of lust and guilt. I thought of Ruth and pulled myself from her and dived under the water. But the image of Melinda, with the sensations that had accompanied it, had scorched themselves on me. I knew I would remember that thrilling sequence as an old man, and I screamed in delight from the sea floor. Big bubbles declared by happiness. When I came to the surface, I knew that Melinda would be slipping back to the shore. I was right.

We dried ourselves with stray towels. The Kermit on hers folded and vanished as she rubbed at her hair, but she kept smiling. There seemed an endless pause, a desert of uncertainty as I tried to plot the course of my conversation with her. We orbited one another like tiny planets. "Where are you going to go now?" she asked, at the last moment.

The partygoers were dispersing, and I knew I had seconds to answer.

"Back to River's," I said, with a pride and pomposity that made me feel both childish and superhuman.

"Come to Seaview beach on Tuesday night," she said. "We're having a barbeque."

"What time?"

Her friend appeared, with a matriarchal smile, and pulled her by the elbow away from me. "I don't know," she said. "Late. See you then?"

Chapter Thirty-One

Seagrove Bay was empty. As I walked along it, I was sure there was a shift in the air, as if summer was being ushered away for another year. An invisible envelope in the air seemed to have closed. The beach was empty, except for a family of blonde-haired women, packing away a barbeque. The water was sloshing hard up against the sea wall with an aggression I hadn't seen before. It was almost as if summer had never happened.

I wondered how I'd finish the walk through the bay to meet Melinda. It seemed a long way away and I didn't even know what I was expecting when I got there, a girl that I'd had one proper conversation with? What if she had forgotten her invitation, or worse, laughed at me for taking it seriously? On the bus ride back to his house, River informed me that Ruth and him were having a dinner party that night with their parents. It was said in a way that had made it clear I was persona non grata. I hadn't pushed my luck any further. I was already concerned he would exaggerate what had happened between Melinda to taunt Ruth, and I was disappointed with myself for giving him such leverage over me. But between a night alone on the beach or one with company, I decided it would be absurd not to make an effort.

As I passed the houses overlooking the bay, I saw a man sat in a deckchair in front of his house with his feet up. He looked so tanned, so at ease with his place in the world. I asked myself if I'd ever feel so relaxed with who I was. What choices had he made to get to that point?

As I approached the bay, I realised I had been missing a great party that I had, this time, been invited too. As I started to pick out the distant silhouettes, frolicking on the sand and

179

running down to the sea, a cloud passed, and the sun threw a golden blast over this patch of the beach and right into my eyes. The effect this moment had on me was really peculiar. It was as if a ball of soothing white had been placed in my stomach. In the stinging glare, I could just make out a row of women in white dresses that were surrounding a small fire. They were like a holy crescent of backlit figures, blonde and luminescent. Like a row of flowers opening, they all opened their arms as I approached. These slender, angelic figures seemed the personification of the spirit of late summer.

As I squinted through the sun, I realised that far from wondering who this intruder was, they were all smiling at me in anticipation. The delicious smell of grilled meat wafted towards me. I could hardly believe my luck. As I got closer and silhouettes grew features, I realised that the closest smile belonged to Melinda.

The party seemed to have calmed her, lifted her. "Jeff!" she said, opening her arms. "You made it!" She pressed a cold beer into my hands. I looked across her at the other women in white, tending to the fire, rushing to find me food. They all seemed to have a beauty I had never noticed before. I had seen all of their faces at some point over the summer, but they had never looked so tanned, animated, so loose, so mellow. Something in their faces had transformed. Could it just have been the work of the summer, or was it the clarity of this evening light? It was a light that was so pure that it seemed impossible to imagine it had never existed.

The women pressed burgers and hot dogs into my hands. They rushed to offer me napkins and fussed over whether I wanted a drink. I sat on a rock as they all looked to me with warmth and concern. As I thanked them, they all hugged me, and were so tender and beautiful that I felt moved.

The circle closed around me. I tried to work out if their gazes to me were maternal, or curious- or what they were. But even the festering paranoia in my mind couldn't sully this pure moment.

Perhaps it wasn't that I had never been invited, but more simply that I had never turned up. Could I have had a whole summer of this, a summer of feminine benediction, spent eating tasty food by an evening sea, a summer of relaxing with a cold beer, by the soothing waves? As I ate, in a state of near ecstasy, I realised I hadn't appreciated how ravenously hungry I was.

Chapter Thirty-Two

The following morning I walked to River's house. I had left the party when Melinda's parents had arrived to take her away, and undertaken a long walk in the purple dark back to my spot on the beach. I had slept deeply that night, for some reason the buzzing mosquitos and the beat of the ocean had not stopped it being the best sleep I had had all summer. It was as if, after years of fantasising about waking up to the sea, I had finally adjusted to the reality of it and something deep inside me had clicked into place. As I walked into River's driveway, the confidence I had gained from the applause last night, and from the swim with Melinda, was still buzzing around my fingertips as I rang the bell.

I waited in the driveway for him to answer the door and caught a glimpse of a shadow moving in a window on Ruth's floor. River pulled the door open and asked me to take my shoes off before flinging himself inside. I tried to convince myself that there was nothing unusual about that, nor in the silent way he obsessed over a bass line as we tried to figure out a song in the living room. At one point I muttered something about needing the loo and I went upstairs.

As I passed Ruth's bedroom door, I offered a tentative 'Hello', but got no reply. But as I stepped downstairs, I heard a movement in her room.

After an hour of frustrated attempts to jam, in which River and I had seemed like we were on different planets, I asked whether Ruth was okay.

He looked out at the garden. "Yeah, she might be a bit mad at you."

"Why?"

River put his head down and tried again to play a bassline

that I knew was beyond him.

"Why would she be mad at me, River?"

He pulled a face. "I don't know, Jeff, and I don't care. Why don't you ask her?"

"Well you do know, River. Because I haven't said anything that might upset her."

He didn't answer as he put his bass closer to his ear.

"River?"

He threw down his plectrum and flashed a glance up the stairs. He leaned forward and said in a bitter stage whisper, "She was asking me all these questions about you at that party." He started looking for his plectrum. "I might have mentioned you and Melinda."

"And why would you do that?" I said. "Especially when nothing happened."

He didn't answer. I leaned back.

"I'm not happy about this, mate," I said.

"Maybe it's for the best," he said. He looked up but wasn't quite able to meet my eye. "It's not as if you and I are having artistic differences anyway. Is it?"

I found myself staring at him for a good few seconds. In the end I said, "I'll be back in a minute."

He pretended not to notice I was going upstairs. I knocked on Ruth's door. "I know you're there. I'm not sure what River has told you, but I think he might've made things sound worse than they were."

I heard a loud bang downstairs. I opened the door. The creak was so loud it was ridiculous.

"Ruth?"

She was sat on the side of her bed, reading a book that had countless luminous markers poking from it.

"What is it?" she asked, without turning.

"River twisted my arm into going to that party. I had a few drinks with various people and stayed up talking until late. I fell asleep on a couch on my own." She turned to look out of the window. "And the next day we all went for a swim."

"Yeah, I heard."

"Nothing happened."

183

Was she wincing? I knew it wasn't the greatest story to tell someone you'd just lost your virginity to.

"I know it all sounds weird but…"

She turned. Her eyes were red, and her skin looked very pale. "You don't think it's bad enough to have River gleefully tell me about you romping around with some girl, do you?"

"I don't know what he told you."

"I know that what he told me sounded a lot worse than all that. And I know I asked him a lot of questions." Her hand flashed up to her brow. "He'd have *loved* that. It sounds like he made the most of it."

"Well, I have been a prick," I said. I walked closer to the bed and sensed that I had to close this wound right now, or I'd regret it. "Ruth, to be honest…"

Was I really going to say what I wanted to say? Judging from the mood in the room I felt I had no choice. Something else in the air was closing. "I really think you've saved my life this summer. I'd have been so lost without you. I don't know what I'd have done."

She looked up at me. Her expression seemed a mix of sympathy, pain and confusion. "Oh, Jeff," she said.

"And also…" I dropped my voice. "What happened the other night means so much to me. I hadn't ever done that before."

Her eyes widened. I started to believe that I might be getting somewhere.

"My head has been a mess this summer," I continued. "And…" I checked River wasn't listening, "I've felt *so* alone."

For a moment I did want to cry, but I stopped myself. Just about.

"And when anyone has paid my attention, I've felt stupid turning it down. I haven't known what to do."

She smoothed the sheet beneath her. "You've had a lot on your plate this summer, Jeff. I didn't think it was fair for your parents to leave you to deal with it all. I was trying to take some things off that plate, but now I wonder if I've been trying to add more to it." She looked past me, out of the window. "Perhaps that was selfish of me."

"No. I've been selfish."

"Yes," she said, her tone flat. "You have. But you haven't been taught any better."

"I know enough to know I care about you. Very much."

"I know," she said. She looked at me. "It's just been a crazy summer." She forced a smile onto her lips. "And let's just leave it at that, shall we?"

"What do you mean?"

Her eyes stayed fixed on a crease in the sheets. "I think it's probably time you left, Jeff."

I put my head down and went downstairs. I had never felt so hollowed out. I had been alone all summer and then the one time someone had crossed the ravine to reach me I'd just broken the bridge.

In the back porch I looked for my trainers. I could only see one of them, and amongst my mental fog I couldn't locate the other. I went through all River's trainers in the box by the door but then I became paranoid that Ruth would hear me and think I was refusing to get out of their house, or River would come down and destroy me. And so in the end I just decided to go bare foot out into the world, get my stuff from the beach and then, I didn't know what then. I had no idea, but I had to go.

There was a figure opening the gate as I began to tread barefoot on the gravel. With a lurch in my stomach I realised I recognised the sandy blonde hair, somehow thicker than before. The eyes were darker, more embedded in some place that I hadn't been.

"Hello, darling," she said, looking up.

"Hi, Mum," I said.

She looked as if she was intending to turn completely towards my body, but that something was stopping her. Her creased linen suit looked new. Her tan was so deep that it had layers, it evoked a range of time zones. She looked like a new person. I wondered if relentless New Age therapy might improve people after all.

"I left a message with River that I was coming to get you. He must've not said "

I felt something move in the upstairs window. The only

thing on my mind was Ruth, and perhaps where to sleep. I didn't know what to say to this foreign creature. I could see her chasing my expression, trying to find a strand of my consciousness to grab.

"I'm not angry with you, darling. Don't worry."

As I looked up at her, I felt something simmer in my eyes. "I don't care if you are angry with me, Mum. I haven't seen you in weeks. And I needed to. Maybe you don't get that. Maybe you're not like me. And you're not like…" I had to say it. "Emma."

She opened her mouth and a wordless sound of regret came out. Her hand flashed to the corner of her mouth. "Oh, Jeff," she said. She stepped forward and took me in her arms. Her shoulders smelled of lavender and talc. "I'm so sorry," she said, into my hair.

"It's okay," I answered, but I could feel wetness from my eyes leaking onto her tissue like top.

"Actually, it's not," a voice said.

I realised Ruth was standing behind us.

My mum released me. "Ruth, dear. I thought it was you. Have you been looking after Jeff?"

I looked up. Ruth had her hand on her hips, her shadow a long, bent shape that passed over mine and my mother's feet.

"Someone had to," she said. "He couldn't face living around people he didn't know this summer. So he spent most of it sleeping on the beach. And that was where he was living until…" She gestured at the bandage, which seemed at that moment very big and absurd.

I looked at my mother. As she saw the bandage for the first time, she opened her mouth and this horrible sound came out. I could see in the jagged path of two tears from each eye a shape of everything that had happened. Not just now but going back to Emma, all their arguments, that time in the car when we met Emma in the hospital, those months at the end that I still couldn't really recall.

I could see, just then, in the flicker of her eyes, how many panicked days she had spent trying to work out how to reach Emma and how to get past how hurt she'd been by her. And

186

how, when she'd died, it had all been so beyond her worst nightmare that there had been nothing left in her to try and reach me this summer. She looked down at the gravel, caressed her own hands, and then looked up.

"Thank you," she whispered to Ruth.

"Yeah," Ruth said.

She turned and went back inside.

My mum took my hand. It felt cold and small. "Okay. Let's get you home," she said.

Chapter Thirty-Three

I was now thirty-four-years-old and hadn't visited Camden since Emma's gig at The Purple Turtle. Ruth and I got off the Tube at Camden Town and, as I caught my reflection in the glass window of the door, I could see the effect of the years on me. I no longer had that anaemic, slender innocence. I now had some bulk; it was almost as if flesh incorporates the experiences we gather and uses them to shore us up. I knew now, for instance, that this was the nearest stop to The Purple Turtle. There would be no getting lost today.

As we pushed through the sweaty crowds, I saw a man sleeping, on a splayed cardboard box amongst the chaos of the exit. Commuters stepped around the complex arrangement of possessions that ensured he kept everything he owned close by. Since when had people accepted their fellow man having a home without walls? I thought of that teenage summer-before mortgages, before leases, before tenancies, when an opulent home had been available to me but when I'd chosen instead to sleep on a beach. How ungrateful I'd been. How unaware I'd been, as well, that it was the choices made in my mind that really mattered. I had to create my own sense of meaning because the outer world not only couldn't, but it had never said it would.

That was the summer I'd learned people could be a refuge too. As Ruth dropped money I offered in the man's cup, I remembered it was her who had taught me that.

It had taken years of silence between us for her to finally reply to my email, for the intervening years to melt away, during late night phone calls and endless messages in which it was all unspooled, at last. We'd told each other everything we'd wanted to tell each other at the time, when it had still felt too hot to touch. Those aching years had taught us what feelings were worth holding onto. They had shown us, as well, which feelings would fall away. In a way it felt like all of that had led to this.

As we kept walking, I thought of how those people on the island had been so dismissive of their luxury homes. Suddenly I could see why, when some people had so little it didn't really make sense for others to have quite that much. Perhaps they had known that they were squandering luxury on themselves and it had made them dislike who they were.

Ruth and I had first talked about making this trip to visit Emma's haunts soon after she had started speaking to me again. It had been her suggestion, one that at first that I had not taken seriously. But it had taken root. During our late-night chats, her at one end of the country, me at the other, we had talked a lot about ghosts. She had once said that, a person was nothing more than a place where their ghosts exist. It had seemed a line she was proud of, so I didn't dismiss it. But as I went about my work, lecturing at the university and working on my first novel, I thought a lot about that comment. In a sense, Ruth and I both had Emma living somewhere inside us. This trip felt, in some strange way, like a meaningful thing to do.

In the intervening years I had picked up one or two things. I had accepted that most people were just trying to fill their days, as if their sheer potential was a burden. Ruth had remarked that it was possible to fill your life with acts we found meaningful, even if everyone around you felt they were absurd. We had decided that this trip fell into that category.

I looked at her with a passion I still couldn't quite express. Perhaps it wasn't just passion, it was gratitude too. She wore a red mackintosh over a printed dress, and tugged at the hood of it as rain threatened to fall. I pulled out an umbrella and placed it over her head. "Thanks," she said, wincing.

As we looked for The Purple Turtle, it occurred to me that so often in life, as we move around the stage set of this world, we feel as if we are trying to create a sense of truth about what we do. We use rituals and dates, and we imbue events with significance, all as part of our desperate attempt to make life feel real. But perhaps the only real is our private communion with a personal sense of meaning? As we walked down the pavement, I felt privileged to be doing this, with *her* of all people. How many negotiations and obstacles had been overcome before Ruth and I could do this?

I remembered the bottleneck, that time we had had met up after so many years, when we both had so much to say. In that deserted café in Portsmouth, overlooking the dock, there had been no code, no protocol, to allow us to unravel it all. Ruth was too smart to accept anything other than the truth and the truth was I hadn't known what that was until I'd asked some searching questions. I felt fortunate to have someone to helped me answer them.

Walking past the stalls, the t-shirts now emblazoned with different jokes, different band names, I felt, in a way that I hadn't since my adolescence. It was as if, for once, life was feeling significant in the moment it occurred. Now Ruth and I were back together, now we were *here*, I felt the significance of the ages swinging in our every step. It was like a melody, playing behind the stage set.

Even in the rain she was as beautiful as she had ever been, her rich, dark eyes, her sensual, deliberate movements. Yet now, for being at my side after we had gone through so much, she was more than that. She was a companion through the ages, through all the misguided years. I felt as if those years had resolved because she was at my side. And for all that this visit felt worthwhile, I also knew it was drenched in nostalgia. I simply had to re-visit the place I had first seen Emma perform.

The Purple Turtle was still there. Walking inside I could see that the bright colours of the Britpop era had faded to the muted tones of the present in which every aspect has been work shopped to within an inch of its life. Menus propped up against counters and price lists set over bars now seemed to have an intensity to them, which I didn't remember them having last time. The spontaneity of the nineties was long gone, a time when optimism and hedonism seemed like proper solutions, leading to a present in which all alternatives now felt exhausted. Now there was just an echo of the times in which hedonism was something to believe in.

As if on cue, I saw a sticker for Rosary pasted onto a girder. Someone had tried to rip it off and its red had faded, but it was still just about there. I remembered how they'd been dropped after their first album. The last anyone had heard of Adam he had been working in a mobile phone shop. It seemed ironic that it was Emma's finally released debut that had gone platinum and not his, given how dismissive he'd always been about her, and how inferior she'd felt to him. All those tracks she had crafted over, and all those songs she had scraped together to record, had been sold by her tiny record label to a larger one. The album had sold more than any of the bands who had deliberately made her feel intimated when she was alive. It had all been worth it, every minute of making music that she had thought no one would hear. Every scratchy recording, where she re-recorded some guitar part because it wasn't quite right, despite her sense that it was pointless. So many people feeling trapped in their bedrooms had taken those distant notes to their heart. Despite how lost I now knew she had felt, every second of her life had counted. It was a lesson I was not going to forget.

We looked around. The black floor was still sticky and the stage that Emma had once occupied was empty. But in the middle of it was the unattended microphone stand. No voice filled the room. It seemed absurd to believe Emma had ever even existed let alone that she had sung here. As Ruth held my hand, I found myself thinking about all the performances that must have taken place in here, all the songs, evoking lifestyles that never came to pass. I thought of all the nights, in the interim, that I had I watched performances of bands from that era, on TFI Friday, or Top Of The Pops. As a teenager I had questioned what the flamboyance of a certain singer, or the sparkle of a certain costume, had revealed about the world, what it revealed about me. But where had all that potential gone? Surely it made sense to revisit that feeling, to try to clear those paths to the present.

"So what was she like at the gig?" Ruth asked, turning to me. "Was she any good?"

I recalled the sheer sense of raw excitement. To see someone made of the same stuff as me making something happen, being spontaneous.

I paced around the room just below the stage, re-living the moment Emma had walked onto it. I remembered the sense of dread that there had been about her impending performance, the assertive, yet abashed way my sister had looked out at the crowd and tried to pick out Mum and me. "Good question," I said, relishing the space opened up by another's intrigue. It was the only place, related to the grief, that I could control, one in which I could feel as if I was ushering Emma to her final home. "She sang this song about how Princess Diana being dragged down Kensington Street would be a fitting end to her funeral."

"Jesus," Ruth said, with a small smile.

"Well exactly. It smacked of…" I paced around, started again. "She spent the whole night pushing boundaries, and that was the moment she transgressed them. I had this sense of…" I could feel myself being expressive with my hands, carving lost faces in the air. "I remember thinking that she was a pioneer, that she was going to places before I did." I exhaled. "She went to loads of places before I did."

I laughed and traced the line Emma had entered the stage from. "She shocked to get people's attention. But at the same time, she was showing people how sharp she could be."

"Sharp? As in cutting?"

I nodded.

"As if anyone doubted that," Ruth said, turning towards the vacant audience. "I wonder, in time, if that sharpness would've got blunted one way or another. It sounds like you were seeing the sharper edge of her that night."

I looked to where she had stood.

Ruth followed my eyes. "I don't know what we're supposed to do," she said.

"To not be here," I answered. "Because it's a bit odd that we are."

192

"I don't know. Maybe you should stand right where she stood, or something."

I loved the trace of humour around her lips. She had on her face an expression that rendered whatever we were about to do okay, because it would 'be funny'. I remembered when we first started dating the way she would get me to do things. She'd say, "Do you think it might be funny if you jumped in the fountain?" The problem was, in the mood we were creating between the two of us, the answer was almost always yes.

"Do you think it'd be funny?" I asked.

She looked away, trying to hide her laugh.

Something about the idea appealed. I went up the stairs and onto the stage, encouraged by the indifference of the bar staff.

It occurred to me I was like a pathologist at the scene of the crime, and people somehow know when the body language of someone is too reverent to be disturbed. For some reason, I felt unable to stand exactly where she had stood.

I stood beside it, in a manner reminiscent of those who leave an empty chair at the dining room table for the departed. Without occupying her space this allowed me to see from where she had seen.

In a sense, this is as far as we can go, isn't it? Back to where the trail ends. From there we look from the vantage point of those who stood there. We can try and work out what they saw, and then try to figure out where they went. You can then decide. Do I want to go there as well?

I knew now that the answer was no. I'd learned that back when self-destruction had seemed unavoidable. I now knew it wasn't unavoidable at all. You just needed the imagination to figure out more options. So the question was, why did she go that way? Why did she decide that was the best path to follow?

In a flash, the answer came to me. "I needed to feel wanted."

I had no idea where that phrase came from. But at that moment I had such a sense of certainty about why she had done what she'd done. It was as if she was whispering it into my ear

She had done what she had done because she needed to feel

wanted and because no-one at home, no-one in any of those rich homes, had been making *anyone* feel wanted. All the enquiries in the world would never conclude that, but I knew that was the real reason Emma had died.

I found myself listening in for any more phrases that might just appear in my head. But there was nothing. Only the swiping of the bar maid's cloth on the bar. Back and forth.

I realised I hadn't felt wanted, not for most of that summer. I had even dismissed Ruth's attempts to reach out to me. I had spent the summer lingering around empty, spooky, beautiful places, trying to find something. The love I was looking for had been on offer. I just hadn't been open to it. Emma had taught me, through diary pages that carried so much emotion that they punctured the pages, how we had to be open to people, sensitive to people. She had described so well how it felt to not be treated with care. I thought of the time I had persuaded her to be more sensitive to Mum. However much Mum had run away from me in the aftermath, in the end she was just another person who was hurting.

I stood there for a while, until Ruth got up on the stage and looked with me. Her fingers wove into mine.

"I suppose this is kind of where the trail ends, Jeff," she said, separating her fingers from mine.

I felt moisture build in my eye. It grew into a plump tear that splashed on my cheek. I was shocked by it, and by how Ruth didn't even pretend to not see me wipe it away. She followed the gesture with what seemed to be passionate curiosity. There was no way this moment wasn't real, wasn't significant. The novelty of that feeling was nourishing.

So much about the venue was as it had been, the scent of lager rising from the sticky floor, the smell of trapped sweat, the shining ceiling, the grim glimmer of optics from behind the bar, the distant black spiral staircase spiralling up to the balcony. The only aspect that was absurdly, cruelly absent, was her. Where were all the appendages to her presence that she'd promised during her performance? What did you do with the band logo now? How did you meet the band? All of it was gone, gone, gone.

In the years after that summer I had diligently gathered together a lot of her writings and journals and made notes of the parts I thought people would most appreciate. I wasn't sure what I was curating them for, but knew one day it would make sense. Her old head mistress got in touch and asked if I had anything of Emma's that I might like to share with the school. There was now a small corner of the school library dedicated to Emma's life and work, the framed platinum disc of their debut record, photos of her first gigs, some of her essays. Most potently of all, there were some of the lyrics she'd scrawled during those sunless years when she was sure no-one cared. All of them were now preserved under the glass. I'd had messages from people telling me they'd travelled from all over the world to her school to see them. So many women told me she had inspired them to form bands. Emma was more loved than she'd ever appreciated. The thought of her energy living on had prevented me from thinking that all that was left of her was fading scraps. To know she had inspired people was wonderful, but it did make me miss her all the more.

But just when the craving for her got so strong that I felt I would scream, something shifted in me. In a panic, I met Ruth's eye.

"What is it?" she asked.

"I feel like she's here," I said.

I didn't know why I'd said it, but the moment I said it I felt as if a lot hung on Ruth's reaction.

"Well…in a way, Jeff," she said.

"No," I said, looking at the microphone stand. "I feel like she's *literally* here."

Ruth looked at the bar, then back at me. Some wager in her brain seemed to have resolved. Our relationship had always been predicated on us opening, rather than closing, our minds.

"Right," she said, squeezing my hand.

I couldn't explain it. I felt like there was a white heat around the spot where Emma had been. It was as if by stepping there I would be stepping into *her*.

Ruth leaned forward. "So what do you want to say to her?" she asked me.

"Christ. I don't know," I said.

Ruth stepped back. "Try to think," she said. "Or…" she flashed a look at the bar. "Just listen."

I did. To my surprise, in that moment, some clear sentiments formed in my mind. They were wordless, but they carried with them an intent that wasn't mine. A will that I recognised coming outside of myself. "I'm sorry," it said.

I touched the microphone stand, the tip, where the microphone would've been. Something inside me that had been bending for many years and threatening to snap, finally did. A man at the bar was looking at me with naked concern. I found myself looking down at the floor. "You didn't need to go," I whispered. "He really wasn't worth it."

I felt the words 'I know', form in my mind. They were clear and sad, like the last breeze of summer. I remembered that feeling, the one she had generated in me during our best days. There was so much love behind those words, so much acceptance, humour and grace. I felt loved, I felt wanted. I felt that whatever pain, confusion and emptiness was in my life would pass. Those sentiments in my mind were so clear, that I felt sure.

I told her that a band, made up of another group of young girls, had used one of her songs and that it had been a hit. I told her it had even been played on Top Of The Pops. I told her that those girls from her school who had made fun of her by shouting, "Top Of The Pops!" that night she had played at the inn had been wrong to laugh at her, because there was now a corner of her old school dedicated to her. I told her about all the messages I'd got from people about her work. And after a long pause I thought I heard something like laughter, and again those words. "I know." And after a moment I got something else. "I'm always here if you need me," it said. "I'm only a few steps away."

I felt so grateful. So happy, and sad, and grateful.

Then that was it. She was gone.

Ruth led me outside. On the pavement outside afterwards we turned our faces up to the sun. "So do you think that was worthwhile?" Ruth asked. "Do you feel any better?"

How could I explain what had just happened?

Did I need to?

"Yeah, I think so," I said.

She took my hand. "So what do you think you've taken away from all this? Anything?"

"Yeah." I smiled. "I suppose I've learned not to let another person dictate my life. No-one is worth dying over. Not in any way." I looked at her. "I'm not going to fall apart over *people*. Not when there's so much to do."

Ruth looked back at the entrance. "Well, I think she taught me that as well," she said. "Now let's go."

Book Club Questions

- Is it the male voice, or the female voice which is more predominant in the novel do you think?

- Jeff seems to be straining to bring his sister back to life by immersing himself in the personal effects she left behind (her diaries, her music, videos of her performances). To what extent can an author bring a character to life using such means?

- What does Jeff seem to think of his sister, Emma? Is his view of her rose-tinted?

- Why do you think Jeff and River have a bond?

- How did Emma seem to view her younger brother?

- How does Emma use her diary in a manner that is perhaps unusual?

- The novel explores what people leave behind, in the form of diaries and artistic legacy. To what extent can the materials people leave behind be explored in the novel form?

- Various figures, from Ophelia to Frances Farmer, Emily Dickinson and Courtney Love influence Emma. What links them, do you think?

- Emma has some strange, otherworldly experiences. To what extent did you think the novel captured the mindset of a creative person like her?

- The effects of heroin use are to some extent explored. Why are characters, in the type of scenes depicted in the novel, perhaps more susceptible to it?

- Beyond her associating Jeff with her sister, what draws Ruth to him?

- How does Ruth see Emma? In what way is Emma influential to her?

- To what extent does Jeff's mum progress as the novel advances?

- How do you think the older generation are depicted in "Dead Rock Stars" and did you think it a fair portrayal?

- In the opening scene, as he sees her perform live, Jeff writes, 'I begin to see how hard Emma has worked, building the world of her music.' To what degree do you think in the nineties there were more mediums by which a musician like Emma could express themself?

- How far does the novel go to portray aspects of the nineties? In what ways does the world seem to have changed in the final section?

Fantastic Books
Great Authors

darkstroke is
an imprint of
Crooked Cat Books

- Gripping Thrillers
- Cosy Mysteries
- Romantic Chick-Lit
- Fascinating Historicals
- Exciting Fantasy
- Young Adult
- Non-Fiction

Discover us online
www.darkstroke.com

Find us on instagram.
www.instagram.com/darkstrokebooks

Printed in Great Britain
by Amazon

64679161R00123